Family Treasure

A Novel

Jessica Tastet

Publications

Family Treasure
Copyright 2018 Jessica Tastet
Cover Design by Ashley Comeaux-Foret

ISBN 978-0-9986173-5-0
ISBN 978-0-9986173-4-3

For my Family,
Who make life interesting.

Twenty-Two Years Ago
Harper

His hands were grubby and sweaty as they closed around her ring. Harper didn't like it none, but she'd agreed to it, and she couldn't go back now or he'd call her a baby, or worse. Then, she'd have to punch him, and his grandpa had told him he couldn't hit girls, so it would be unfair really.

"You look like your rabbit just died all over again, Harper." Sissy had her arms crossed with her two braids flapping over the collar of her Peter Pan shirt. She always had to dress pretty, even when they were on an adventure out under the moon way past their bed times. People called her Prissy Sissy sometimes, but Harper didn't let that slide. Only she could call her that, and she only did that when Sissy wouldn't play with her because the girl didn't want to get dirty. Then she figured it was a nickname she deserved.

"You're going to get it back," Emmett said, dropping it into a wooden box where it fell between a set of jacks and an ice cream eraser. "I promise."

"I better." She swallowed against the aching in her throat. "I paid my own coin for that today, and I didn't get to wear it even a whole day."

"You don't even like jewelry," Sissy said haughtily, her lips pursed. She'd been angry when she'd only received a rainbow puff sticker out of the machine, and Harper had received the ring she'd coveted from the glass bubble as they'd waited their turns. Truthfully, Harper had thought she'd give it to Sissy eventually, but she was waiting until Sissy had something she wanted in trade.

As they reached the edge of the garden, Harper spied Granddaddy leaning on his shovel in the moonlight, his gloves now tucked in his back pocket.

His eyes seemed to twinkle under the moon as he looked at them with a grin, giving credence to Harper's thoughts that her granddaddy was magical. "Did we find some treasure to bury?"

"Yes, Sir." They all chimed together.

Emmett shook the box and the items clattered all about. Harper could tell him not to go and mess it all up, but she decided not to ruin the moment.

Granddaddy waved his free hand over the hole. "Well, let's sink the treasure box in the ground so we can have our own buried treasure story."

Lying on his belly, Emmett placed the box into the deep hole. It looked lonesome in the dark cave of the dirt. Harper picked up a handful of dirt and tossed it over the box, dirtying the old wooden treasure chest they'd scavenged from the attic.

The splatter of dirt reminded her of something out of *Treasure Island* or Granddaddy's pirate tales. He was the best storyteller she knew—better even than Mama who always ruined the endings.

Another handful of dirt bounced against the wood, and when she looked up, Emmett grinned at her revealing his missing tooth. They were two pirates, burying their treasure for later. But the third one needed to join in or there would be mutiny.

"Come on, Sissy," Harper said turning toward the cross Sissy. "Your turn."

"You're nuts if you think I'm going to touch dirt," Sissy said, stomping her foot. "I painted my nails pink today, and they are not touching nasty mud."

"Don't be like that, Sissy," Harper said. "We made a pact."

"Use the shovel," Emmett said, tossing his head toward Granddaddy.

Granddaddy held the shovel out, and Sissy hesitated, twiddling with her pink fingernails. In the end, though, she took it and tossed a few morsels of dirt down the hole with the tip of the shovel before stepping back.

"Now, I did it," she declared, standing straight with her chin tilted upwards. "Leave me alone about it."

Harper tossed another handful in for good luck, and Emmett laughed and grabbed both hands full and released them over the mounting pile.

"Okay you two," Granddaddy said, chuckling. "Let me get this treasure buried before Grams discovers us out here, and we have to dig more holes."

Harper giggled and dropped another fistful in before stepping away from the box and the pit. The night air felt hot and moist, like a heavy, wet blanket, but one that tingled with an electrical current. She wished she and Emmett could race to the old barn like they would if it was daylight, but they'd promised

Granddaddy to behave with only burying treasure tonight.

Sissy tapped her foot on the grass, blowing a breath hard up her face, rustling her bangs. "So how long are we going to leave the treasure down here?"

Harper twirled around, keeping her eyes on Granddaddy shoveling the dirt to enclose the box each time she spun around. "Long enough to forget where it's at."

"That's silly," Sissy said, crossing her arms.

Emmett patted Sissy on the arm, his eyes soft with concern. "Don't worry, Sissy. I have a map."

Sissy shrunk away from him, swiping at her sleeve where he'd touched. "Ugh. Your hand's all dirty."

"Stop being such a baby," Harper said, bumping into Sissy to let her know she needed to relax. Sissy grimaced, but her shoulders drooped some. Turning to her granddaddy, she thought of his favorite bedtime story for her. "Granddaddy, it will be just like the family treasure, right?"

Granddaddy chuckled, but he paused in his digging and surveyed the grounds of the Ames land. "Except you will have a map, so we will know how to find it when you are ready."

Emmett clutched the construction paper, crayon-drawing map to his chest. "I will guard it with my life."

"You better, Emmett Hebert," Harper said. "I want my ring back one day."

Part I

Harper

Harper Ames veered around a gawking group standing still on the sidewalk, maneuvering her way through the midmorning crowds of Magazine Street. She needed to hurry. Leaving Tara waiting too long in a wedding dress shop would come with consequences. She'd choose the most hideous dress and have it all bagged up just to pay Harper back for the experience. This was not her morning though. And of course to add to the delay, she'd had to park two blocks away.

Her phone vibrated in her pocket, and she put it to her ear as she sidestepped the uneven pavement.

"I'm on my way, Tara," Harper said, the people's faces blurring as she hurried past. "I think I left my wallet at the bakery since I can't find it this morning."

"Harper, is that you?" Grandmother Patsy asked, an uncertainty catching her voice.

Drats. She hadn't looked at the screen, only assumed Tara's impatient rant would await her on the other end. Recently, she'd been avoiding Grams's calls. More like putting off returning them with one excuse or another. She had been working long hours and then there was the wedding planning that must be done quickly now that Clint wanted to pull it off before they had to move.

Harper stopped to catch her breath a moment, allowing a group of tourists to cross in front of her. Sweat had begun to bead at the nape of her neck from her mad sprint. That would not be pretty trying on white gowns. How did you even get sweat stains out of white satin or silk? Another worry to add to the ever-growing list.

"Grams," Harper responded. "It's good to hear from you."

"I've been trying to call you," Grams said, her tone chastising. "I thought you might have changed phone numbers."

"Oh, no, Grams," Harper said, continuing at a walk instead of a sprint. "The bakery's busy at this time of year, and we've taken on more weddings than usual."

"That's good, Dear, if you're happy," she replied. Harper didn't know if that lingering question her words seemed to incite was her imagination or intentional on the spry woman's part. "I wanted to talk to you about your granddaddy."

"I've been meaning to call him." Harper held her breath like she'd done when she was a young girl telling a lie. She released it when she caught herself. It wasn't that she didn't want to call the man that she'd admired so much growing up, but their conversations were painful. There was a sinking terribleness she recognized as fear in the pit of her stomach. Fear that she would call and he wouldn't recognize her voice or remember her name. She didn't know if she could bear it.

"He's getting worse," Grams spoke, her voice a soft, pliable sound. "It's time to come for a visit."

Harper sighed. "I know."

"When?"

"I'll talk to Felipe and see if he can spare me a day or two next week." Harper cringed thinking of the request already. The man baked beautiful cakes and treats, and his king cake season could support them for half the year, but he suffered from poor people skills and preferred for her to take care of anything to do with the clients. He loved people, but they found him rude and overbearing. Something you didn't want when you were trying to draw in business. She'd only managed off today because she'd given him free reign to do whatever he wanted for her wedding cake—a concern she figured she'd sort out later.

"Harper," Grams reproached. "You shouldn't keep putting it off."

Reaching the bakery finally, the closed sign greeted her from the sleek thin glass. Glancing down at her watch, the dial showed 9:22. Twenty-two minutes late for wedding dress shopping, and twenty-two minutes late for the shop to open to customers.

"Let me call you back in a few minutes."

Harper ended the call and dug out the shop keys from inside her purse.

Opening the door, Harper entered the darkened shop. The cakes, cupcakes, and petit fours all welcomed her from the cases, the smell of almond icing bombarding her senses and clenching in her empty stomach.

The metal café tables sat clean and awaiting customers, and the sleek board along the backboard showed the daily offerings and showcased a lemon tart special.

Everything looked as it should, except Felipe should have

opened already. Being neglectful at ordering stock was quite different than forgetting to open at all. Maybe he'd decided to protest her not coming in today after all. No, that was terrible. They'd discussed this. They'd even tossed around the idea of her training someone new again. He'd chased the last five employees off with his nasty outbursts and rude insults, but he would need help soon when she and Clint figured out the future. She'd also considered finishing her history dissertation and actually graduating as she'd planned when she was young and idealistic. Of course, Clint didn't seem thoroughly on board, but that could just be his final medical exams looming and the constant pressure of finding his dream position when he finished his internship in a month. He wanted far away—she wanted nearby. They had some time to figure it out, but Felipe needed every available second to find someone who would remain at the bakery. The job wasn't awful though. It did pay their rent and the wine. Two things Clint didn't want to have to worry about as he completed his dream of becoming a doctor, possibly a surgeon, one day.

Harper walked around the counter and immediately spotted her wallet on the floor. It must have fallen out yesterday when she'd tugged her purse from its slot between the folded boxes and ribbon rolls. When she bent to pick it up, she heard a grunt and then a moan of pain from the back kitchen area.

Fear edged in on her already frazzled emotions. Had Felipe injured himself and been unable to open? Had someone retaliated for a recent tongue-lashing he'd built a reputation upon? It was bound to happen at some point. The man was more grizzly than teddy bear.

Harper approached the black curtained walkway to the kitchen cautiously, unsure of what she'd find and not mentally prepared for anything horrible. She'd only guzzled a half a cup of coffee this morning, and she could feel it jittering around her insides.

Covered with a light dusting of fine white powder, the usual pans cluttered the stainless steel counter. A chocolate concoction with chocolate shavings sat in unfinished glory at Felipe's usual workspace, but no burly salt-and-pepper bearded gentleman stood at any of his usual spots. Just as she turned toward the closet-size office, another groan escaped, causing the hair on the back of her neck to stand up.

It had come from the office, but this sound had a distinctly more masculine tone to it than Felipe's nasally baritone.

Should she leave? Had she interrupted a private moment?

Someone could be injured though. Not opening the shop did not fit with his need to further his business. He'd even promised to call his niece to help out if he thought he couldn't run the front and kitchen.

She should be sure. She'd be upset if something had happened and she'd not checked. Harper edged near the ajar door and peered inside.

A wave of nausea swooshed over her, this morning's coffee bubbling in her esophagus. She should back away.

She wanted to move, to run out of there, but her body would not listen to the rational thought.

Felipe and Clint were sprawled over the white prefab desk, trousers littering the floor.

Clint's face was contorted in the moment of ecstasy that she'd come to know so well over the last six years.

No. Actually he'd never looked so happy. He'd told her it was the stress of medical school and then the hours of being a resident. He'd been distant for a few months, buried in his books, and then last month, he'd decided he wanted to get married right after he finished his internship. He wanted to plan their lives together from that moment forward.

It all rushed through her ears like a revving engine.

She'd been going wedding dress shopping today.

She'd worked for Felipe for five years, putting up with the man's insufferable quirks because he was Clint's oldest childhood friend. Clint had always smoothed things over between the two of them, defended his friend for having had a difficult childhood growing up gay, and Harper had admired that Clint didn't allow that to bother him like some men she knew. She'd grown to think of Felipe as family.

The anger began to warm itself in her center, letting itself awaken.

"How could you?" Harper uttered, disturbing the two finally.

And when they both looked back at her, she didn't know which one she was talking to, the betrayal felt so raw.

Emmett

The cardboard box slipped to the tips of his fingers, but he clung to the corners with a determination to reach the bed with contents intact. He should have packed lighter, but he'd been steadfast in his goal to fit everything in as few boxes as possible to make this move quick. After deciding it was a necessity to return to his grandfather's home and look after things for a while, he didn't want to linger over the choice. Returning home as a grown man stung a bit, but he'd count on the old Band-Aid analogy holding true in this case.

A creak sounded from behind him. He turned to see his grandfather approach the doorway, his hands folded over his thick sweater vest. "Was that the last of them then?"

"I think so Gramps." Emmett glanced around his childhood room. All signs from boyhood had been wiped out when he'd moved out to attend college followed by law school. Grammy had painted the room a royal blue and added sophisticated bedding and curtains. She'd left a few mementos behind like that picture of him with his first big fish at eight years old and a trophy from a tennis tournament he'd participated in during high school. But even they sat on an oak dresser with no dints and dings from the rough boy he'd been. Other than the two boxes of mementos tucked away in the top of the closet, the room didn't speak of the rough, adventurous child he'd been.

Gramps shook his head. "Can't believe you're moving home at your age. In my day, it would be shameful."

Emmett gritted his teeth. He'd known this would be challenging, possibly more so than law school. "It's only for a short time. I need to make sure Winston gets back on his feet, and you need…" He trailed off, catching himself too late.

"I need what?" Gramps asked, puffing up his chest. "I'm an old man, not an invalid. Lottie may have taken care of me for the last fifty-eight years, but it doesn't mean I can't do for myself now that she's gone."

Emmett kicked at the bedpost gingerly, considering an afternoon run. It had been years since he'd actually gone for a rung, but he would need something to deal with the two Hebert men under this roof. "You will need help getting Winston to straighten up, especially if he won't seek help."

Gramps batted his hand in the air, as if he could swat away his only son's alcohol issues as easily as a fly. "Your father will bounce back. Losing the practice will be enough to shake his little problem. A wake up call, so to speak. You can't keep an Hebert down, you'll see."

Yanking the box open, he pulled his alarm clock out and walked around to the nightstand to avoid further comment. He couldn't seem to penetrate the man's blind spot when it came to his son. It didn't matter how low in the black sinkhole Winston dove, his grandfather thought he was doing fine. This inability to see the flaws had not extended a generation toward his grandson. Emmett could never escape the man's harsh criticism.

Emmett glanced back to the man still staring into the room, his eyes looking for something to dislike. He may as well give him a topic to chew on. "Ms. Ames has asked me to talk to you about the feud you and Mr. Walter have going on. After hearing her out, I think you should be the one to end it."

"Never," Gramps said, straightening his spine, sticking his portly belly out. "That insufferable man continues to venture onto my property, and I will not stand for it."

"You won in court. Shouldn't that be what matters?"

"It most certainly does," Gramps said, "which is why he needs to stay off of my property."

After a property line dispute, the two neighbors had ended up in court. Granddaddy had won the ten feet he'd argued belonged to him. As a retired judge, no one would have dared rule against the Honorable Judge Franklin Hebert III. Emmett could see why Mr. Walter still held the grudge over this and other incidents between the families that had never had their day in court.

Emmett pulled several books out of the box. "Perhaps a fence then?"

Gramps jerked back as if slapped. "Why should I have the hassle and expense of a fence? Besides, it would ruin the aesthetic of the property. No, you tell Ms. Ames to keep her husband off of my land."

Emmett shook his head. "I will speak to her again, but I think it such a shame you can't work it out with your neighbors. You were friends once."

Gramps knocked on the doorframe before turning to leave.

"When you finish unpacking, come downstairs for a word with your father. Perhaps now he's feeling up to talks about returning to work."

He didn't wait for an answer before leaving. Pulling a roll of ties from the box, Emmett doubted Winston wanted to talk about work. Maybe if he could find work in the bottom of a bottle, it might be on his mind. Emmett himself had a different color tie for each day at the office, when he'd once been able to practice at the family law firm that is. After a few bad decisions coming off of years of bad choices, his father had been forced to sell the practice to pay off debts and avoid a major scandal. All of this meant that Emmett had gone a few weeks without wearing a tie or filing papers or appearing in court. Winston, his father, had effectively made him unemployed.

Emmett tossed the ties in one of the empty drawers. Funny, he didn't even like ties, but he resented Winston for taking away his routine. Now, he had to start a job search. And live back at home with his stubborn Grandfather and his drunken father.

A large thump and then the crash of something falling over sounded from down the hall. Emmett stood in the middle of the room, considering if he wanted to ignore it or see what Winston had managed now. Emmett had known what he was getting into though, he reminded himself. He needed to get the two Hebert men straight, and it wasn't going to happen without friction – not with those two.

Harper

The old cream Acadian house looked the same as it had since its construction seventy years before. Hanging ferns graced the sweeping, deep front porch while a ficus tree stuffed behind oversized wooden rockers and a coir welcome doormat beckoned her toward the massive oak door that completed the picturesque entry. As Harper's father had often said, nothing really changed in the South—when you returned, it would be just as you left it.

Ever the big-picture man, Harper knew her father's generalization to be only partially true. The pink camellia bushes that had once hidden her for numerous games of hide-and-seek hadn't faired well under the stress of an unusual bout of cold and had been trimmed down to brown twigs to hide all the dead patches. That live oak tree that her mother had planted on Earth Day when she was seven had tilted ten years ago in a hurricane, and its branches now rested on the ground as much as they reached toward the sky. It was as if they were genuflecting majestically to the person who'd planted it as a seedling. A northern transplant, her father had only looked for drastic, quick changes like the changing of a skyline with a glass and iron skyscraper. At her grandparent's home, change came slow and easy like sipping sweet tea on a back porch.

It had been a year since she'd stepped onto this front porch. At least that long. Grams's birthday party on the back verandah. She'd driven in for the night alone because Clint had worked thirty-six hours straight and wanted to sleep. Her grandmother had stood behind her huge almond icing cake, rouge on cheeks, and her favorite pink lipstick shade pursed to blow out the sparkling candles when Harper's glance had slid to her granddaddy's face to see his normal adoration visible in his warm eyes. But there was dullness, a far away look in his gaze. He'd openly puzzled over his wife, unseeing and unknowing for a moment. She'd watched as fear had clouded his eyes only seconds later. The dementia diagnosis had only been words before. A dismissal with "but Granddaddy remembers everything. He called and asked about so-and-so just yesterday."

It hadn't been only words though. It was deposits of protein fragments of plaque and twisted strands of tangles and nerve cell damage and death to the parts of his brain. A clinical explanation Clint had spouted out after her Aunt Effie had called to deliver the diagnosis. What Harper's devastated mind had registered had been the upcoming death to the millions of memories that made up the man that anchored her life to this place. A home that no matter how far she'd trampled away had anchored her drifting spirit.

As she turned the old brass doorknob, she noticed that Grams had a frog planter standing princely near the door. She smiled. A whimsical touch—a nice update to the provincial front porch. Further evidence that things changed one lawn ornament at a time. Nearly colliding into a tall, thin bottle blonde, Harper opened the door as Sissy click-clacked through in heels and a cream-colored pantsuit.

"Why look at you," Sissy said, stepping back and clutching her designer bag tightly against her fitted t-shirt. "Didn't expect to see you here."

"Grams called," Harper said, the distress creeping into her flesh again, tingling through her as with static electricity. Only two hours ago she'd wanted to delay the visit, but when one's world turns upside down and shakes one out of it, one must find a new place to nest while licking the wounds—or in this case, an old place.

"Ah," Sissy said, her thin neck straightening to its tall stance. "She's *been* calling for you, Harper. Nice of you to finally make it."

The two locked eyes with each other a moment, an animosity passing between them that had grown overtime like fermenting wine.

Grams appeared in the grand entry of the house, peering at the two by the door. She looked the same as she had a year ago. Silver hair sprayed into its short updo, thin delicate cheekbones rubbed with pale rouge. "Harper, is that you?"

"I have to run." Sissy said with a smile that did not reach her eyes. "I have to get to the shop to relieve the morning shift. I'm glad you decided to come for a visit finally."

Sissy skittered past Harper clacking by in her heels. Dismissing the judgment of Sissy, she moved into Gram's awaiting arms for the embrace the petite woman waited for with openness. Inhaling baby powder and gardenia inside the nape of the woman's neck, the smells transported her back to crawling into the woman's lap as a young child to learn to work the crochet needles and run her fingers through the wool or silk yarn. She'd grip Grams's hands and mimic the movements as her hands rhythmically weaved the string into fancy stitches.

"You are such a welcome surprise," Grams said, pulling away to stare into her face. "Granddaddy's taking a nap though. I would have kept him awake if I knew to expect you."

Harper shook her head. "It's okay. I've decided to stay awhile, so I'll see him when he wakes. How's he feeling?"

Grams's lips slipped into a straight line. "It's not a good day today, but how about you? How are you managing to stay? What about the bakery and Clint?"

The stress of taking care of Granddaddy had added more stress lines around her eyes and her forehead. Of course, it could be her approaching seventy-sixth birthday. For so long though, the woman had appeared not to age. The petit woman gave off an aura of being larger than life, but that spark felt duller under the weight of her new burden.

Harper could not add to the woman's troubles. Not right now when she didn't know what her next hour would be like, much less the next move of her life. She could delay today's events until she could get them out without feeling as if she would suffocate. She just couldn't bear to speak any of it aloud yet.

"Clint is finishing up his residency and searching for a fellowship position. I've been considering what I will do to finish my own schooling, so I've decided to take some time to weigh my options. This place has always offered me clarity, and besides, I feel like I need to be here."

Harper offered Grams a reassuring smile to add to the believability. In the conversation with herself on the drive here, the story had sounded plausible after she'd worked through several revisions.

After running out of the bakery unable to stand the sight of their faces anymore, and a steady trembling growing through her, she'd torn through the house they rented, tossing items into an overnight bag, unable to focus on what items had made it into the bag. During the midst of this, her phone had rung twice. Once from Clint, the other Felipe; she'd ignored both calls and fled here, her breathing only returning to normal when she'd reached Highway One.

Right now she needed to keep moving forward, even if it felt as though none of it was real. She'd exited her life and moved into the surreal.

"No matter what's the reason, I'm so happy you're here." Grams said, tilting her head and pointing her chin upward at the same time. She may not be quite convinced, Harper thought. "Why don't you bring your things in and get settled while I get some of your favorite brownies in the oven. The ladies are coming over anyway."

Harper's mouth watered at the mention of the woman's made-from-scratch chocolate delicacy. Growing up, that had been the comfort food and the celebration treat. She assumed Grams meant that the quilting ladies who'd attended a quilting session once a week for the last forty years would be joining them shortly. That front study saw more gossip than quilting as far as Harper could tell, but she was glad that her grandmother still had these women in the midst of all Granddaddy's medical issues.

While Grams disappeared into the kitchen, Harper returned to her car to retrieve her suitcase. The Mini Cooper had been a source of contention between her and Clint, as he wanted to keep the old Accord she'd received from her father as a graduation present instead of spending the money, but she'd bought the impractical car anyway figuring she'd sacrificed enough by sitting out and working while he finished school. The suitcase barely fit into the back, but she'd stuffed it along with a backpack containing her dissertation notes, history books, and laptop. Nestled inside her suitcase was also the wine bottle opener that she'd yanked from the kitchen drawer in the only vengeful thought she'd mustered in the chaotic packing.

After half pulling, half pushing the obnoxiously heavy suitcase up the flight of stairs as quietly as she could manage so as not to disturb her granddaddy, she entered her old bedroom, first door to the left. Although she'd never officially lived here, she'd had enough sleepovers to have a room to call her own within these walls. Partially her own, she thought as she stared at the two twin beds covered in blue kaleidoscope patterned quilts. Sissy had often slept to her right, but only when her father allowed. Whereas Harper's life with her mom had been fluid in terms of rules, Uncle Richard had rules in place for everything. Sissy had to split her time equally between grandparents, so if she'd sleep over with her at Granddaddy's, she would have to then spend the night at her grandmother Tate's house. Sissy had silk pajamas at Grammy Tate's and had breakfast served with flowers in a vase, so she didn't complain at all over the hardship.

All of the upstairs rooms served as guest rooms now as all the children and grandchildren were grown. When he came in from

North Carolina, Uncle Russell stayed down the hall in the hunter green tulip quilt room, a room that had once been his bedroom growing up. Twice a year Uncle Phillip brought the family from Shreveport to visit in the orange sunburst room that was also once his. Growing up, Uncle Phillips's room had served as a sleep over room for the boys, even hosting the neighbor Emmett a few times. This was all before they were aware that sleeping over as boy/girl might have different connotations, and certainly before their world had crashed down on them at fifteen. Then, her dad swept her up, moving her across the country to Pennsylvania, turning this room really into a guest room for her.

Wheeling her suitcase over to the rosewood wardrobe cabinet, Harper threw herself across the bed and it squeaked beneath her weight, the same as it had countless times before with those ancient metal springs. Her mother had probably done this before her many times. That thought had always offered a comfort to her.

Which reminded Harper. She reached under the bed and poked around under the metal frame and eventually her fingers touched the edges of a folded page. She tugged gently and it gave way.

Unfolding it, she smiled at the childish loops of letters sprawled across the back of the picture—a Robert Frost quote her mother had put on the wall of their family room growing up. "Home is the place where, when you have to go there, they have to take you in." Her mother's decorating sense would probably be described as whimsical today. She liked what she liked, whether it made sense or not. But even within the odds and ends, Harper had always liked those carefully chosen words.

Turning the photograph over, a blurry snapshot of a moment in time greeted her of when she was ten years old eating watermelon on the back porch surrounded by everyone who she thought would be in her world forever. Her mom and dad sitting in the old metal glider rocker, actually holding hands. She couldn't tell in the picture that there were cracks in their smiles. Had they known as they clasped hands that he'd be done two weeks later? Had they discussed divorce in hushed whispers when Harper wasn't paying attention. She couldn't tell that he'd be gone for the next five years, and she'd only see him twice a year until her mother was gone, and as a stranger he'd arrived to take her away from the life she'd known. The picture only showed their lopsided smiles. Granddaddy sat on his rocker, a piece of watermelon in one hand; the other arm slung over the curved armrest, his hair a mess from the wind. Grams sat in an old bide skin chair that had been a fixture near the back door as long as she could remember. She sat there everyday to put her shoes on, and Granddaddy kept his boots nestled underneath it. Uncle Richard and Aunt Effie sat on the porch near her parents with their legs dangling over the sides. Aunt Effie's dress wafted around her and her hair was curled meticulously; Sissy had been raised by the woman who dressed her best to have afternoon watermelon.

She, Sissy, and Emmett had grinned widely with melon juice dripping down their chins as the picture had snapped. Sissy had wiped the stickiness away as soon as the Kodak had flashed. The three had been friends at this age. They certainly had not known what the future would hold.

Emmett's dad had been behind the camera.

They'd all felt like family back then.

Looking at the picture after all this time, the old anger didn't come rushing back. Certainly not the same tumultuous emotions that had caused her to stick it between the springs at fifteen.

Maybe it had something to do with her draining day or the fifteen years' distance between then and now. She'd like to believe that none of them knew how things were going to end up. She didn't know if she had that much forgiveness inside her since she wasn't feeling particularly gracious today.

The doorbell strummed from downstairs, echoing loudly throughout the house. Harper sat up. Had the ladies arrived already? She'd been looking forward to a brownie first. Rich chocolate could be a great comfort food when one had chosen to hide out and sink into self-pity.

Then, she heard the distinct sound of a male voice, not the familiar baritone of Granddaddy, but someone younger.

Emmett

"Are you sure you don't want a cup of coffee?" Mrs. Ames asked, sliding a pan of rich chocolate into the oven.

Emmett shook his head, considering how many times he'd watched this same scene play out his entire life. "This isn't a social call."

"Nonsense," Mrs. Ames said, reaching into a cabinet next to the sink for an oversized celadon mug. He'd come to think of it as his mug over the last five years of drop-ins. "Every opportunity is a chance to visit."

"Unfortunately, I am the bearer of bad news," Emmett said, fiddling with the saltshaker on the small bistro table near the back windows. "Gramps will not relent and has asked for me to relay that he wants Mr. Walter to keep off the property. I'm sorry I couldn't do more."

Emmett cringed at his pitiful apology, as if it would soften the blow of the news. He hated this rift between the two families, and he straddled both, seeming to not fit neatly into either. In moving back in with his grandfather, he hoped to not just be the buffer but to smooth the ripple out. Although he knew his grandfather could be stubborn, he'd expected to find the words within himself to shore up the divide. He had not summoned that miracle yet.

"Why must he stay off the property?" A voice from the kitchen archway drew him out of his brief self-pity.

Emmett turned to see Harper Ames standing, hand on a curvy hip crinkling a fitted, black t-shirt. She looked thinner than the picture Mrs. Ames had on the front mantle. The blonde streaks that would deepen every summer when they were children had faded some, blending in with her long auburn locks. Her emerald green eyes stared into his, studying him. She hadn't let go of the old anger. It reflected in her eyes. A straight shooter, she'd never hidden anything from him or anyone; her eyes would betray her instantly.

"Everything's alright, Harper," Mrs. Patsy said, setting his mug of coffee down in front of him. To Emmett, she patted him on the shoulder. He hid his smile so as not to add to Harper's suspicions. "Harper has decided to visit for a while. She can help me attend to Walter, so it will be no worry, Emmett."

Harper entered the room and crossed toward the island to fiddle with a fruit arrangement, all to avoid him, Emmett could tell. "What am I helping with?"

"Oh, it's nothing dear," Mrs. Patsy said, fiddling with her own mug at the table, gazing down at the liquid. "Walter has decided he must find the old Ames treasure."

Harper looked up at him again, and their eyes met. He stilled under her gaze. "And why does the judge have a problem with him?"

He could remember a time when he would have tugged her

hair and told her that she was being mean, that her tone revealed her animosity. Once they'd been honest with each other. Having transitioned from childhood best friends to sweethearts hadn't affected this brutal childhood innocence. But bonds did break, and he had to suffer the glare now.

"He's digging holes on my grandfather's property," Emmett said, his fingers thumping against the mug.

"Oh," Harper said, glaring at him for a moment longer before shifting her focus to Mrs. Ames.

Mrs. Patsy smiled, her thin eyebrows rising in response. "He's a very determined man." She then studied her coffee, eyes downcast, shoulders drooping. But, a moment later, she straightened her shoulders and lifted the mug to her lips. Her eyes remained locked on the glass table though.

Harper stared at a spot above his head on the wall behind him, a far away gaze in her eyes. She'd noticed the slight shift. Something else she may blame him for in his multitude of slights. "I'll speak to him. Thank you for letting us know."

Emmett felt a brief surge of anger at his grandfather. With a small amount of compassion, his grandfather could be the bigger person here.

"I'm really sorry, Mrs. Ames," Emmett said.

"I know," Mrs. Patsy said, looking at him. She offered him a smile, but he could see the weariness flicker in her eyes. Mr. Walter was wearing her out.

"I'm going to get going," Emmett said, standing up. "I told Gramps I'd help him figure out the laundry."

Mrs. Ames nodded her head. "I'm sure you'll be a big help in Mrs. Lottie's absence."

He didn't want to disagree with the woman he'd always felt was a second grandmother, so he allowed the comment to pass without response. Emmett ducked out, not glancing at Harper. Truthfully, he didn't want to know what her reflective eyes would reveal. He couldn't stand pity, but her coldness might make him snap.

His grandmother's passing had been a shock. The inevitable nature of death occurring to someone her age had, of course, occurred to him once or twice, but she'd been so healthy. She'd loved gardening and her roses were a source of pride. She'd been a member of the local garden club and the primary organizer of the area's garden tour each year. Once, before all the bad blood, Mrs. Ames and his grandmother had been friends. They'd socialized together, shared recipes, and attended some of the same fundraisers. Vaguely recalling some interesting stories of the two ladies from school, he wished he had paid attention when they were told. Now, after everything, it wasn't okay to ask. As far as Emmett could see from that time, the two didn't have a falling out, and they never displayed any animosity towards each other, but when the husbands feuded, each remained devoted to their husband's side and respected their wishes to sever ties. A decision Emmett couldn't see happening much outside of that particular generation. On principle, he could admire it, although his own loyalty had remained split between the two families.

Emmett's stroll took him through the live oak tree line that served as a property line and through the back portico where the rose bushes grew. They were jutting out in haphazard directions looking a tangled mess against the trellis. His grandmother, Lottie, had called this her sitting garden. A glider swing sat snuggled between two angel statues and more overgrown shrubbery. She hadn't been here to trim everyday for the last seven weeks as she normally did to keep the growth in check or to remove the wilted roses.

It struck Emmett as he looked around, perspiring in the mid-afternoon sun, that if none of the inhabitants of the house took over the tending of Grammy Lottie's garden, they would have to remove all the plantings.

His chest hurt with the same terribleness as it had when he'd found her in the kitchen collapsed, unconscious. Only seconds from death, he was told later as they explained the aneurysm that had burst inside her skull as she'd mixed the ingredients for her blackberry cobbler. She'd invited him over that day, enticing him with his favorite treat. She'd missed him, she'd said over the phone. He'd been avoiding his father; therefore, he also hadn't seen her for the two weeks before her death. Guilt he'd squared away by punishing himself with taking care of the two Ames men. He couldn't let these roses go though.

He rubbed his hair, conscious that he did this when he felt overwhelmed. He knew nothing about gardening. As his father always said, they'd learned nothing about real life from the fancy schools they'd attended.

Harper

The smell of the stew was intoxicating. No matter how much Harper attempted to replicate her grandmother's cooking, she couldn't master the savory blend of spices that denoted the woman's signature dishes. In the year she'd stayed away, she'd dreamed about her cooking, among other things from this place.

"I'm just surprised you have decided to stay," Sissy said, pouring sweet tea into a turquoise-tinted glass filled with ice cubes. "I know with my own café, it's extremely difficult to allow the help to have off for longer than a day or two."

"You have a restaurant now?" Harper asked. "What about the antique store?"

"Of course, I still run that," Sissy said, waving her hand as if Harper had been ridiculous. Granddaddy looked up from his beef stew and stared at her. For a moment, the blankness did not seem to cloud his eyes. He seemed to see her, and his brain appeared to slowly register her words.

"How do you manage both?" Harper asked, hoping that if she continued the topic, perhaps they could lift his "bad day."

"Well, Harper," Sissy said slowly, as if she was talking to a child. "When one manages, one can hire people like *you* to work like you do at that little bakery. I have two baristas who serve coffee for me in shifts at the café. They are hopeless with the sandwiches though, so I also have Albert that works at the antique shop so that I can cook."

"Albert always gets the orders wrong," Granddaddy said. "Yesterday he delivered a blue and white soldier vase and its cover to a customer who'd purchased an old Parish porcelain tea and coffee set. I should fire that fool, but it's difficult to find good help. I'm waiting for my granddaughter to grow up."

"Your granddaughters are all grown up." Sissy's tone was biting.

"Sissy," Grams exclaimed, clutching the blue and white check napkin in her hand tightly, as she'd been about to drape it in her lap.

"That's right," Granddaddy said, looking at each of their faces around the table. His eyes flickered with doubt as they rested on Harper.

Harper's cheeks burned with the anguish of it all. When he'd woken from his nap and came upon her in the sitting room, he hadn't remembered her and had briefly thought she was her mother. Grams had gently explained it to him, and he'd wrapped her in a warm but hesitant hug. She'd whispered that today was a bad day, but that they didn't come every day yet. The devastation of the moment had felt exactly as she'd expected.

"Harper's here." His eyes softened at the corners as he looked upon her. "You're all grown up. How long are you staying?"

"Yes, Harper," Sissy said, grimacing at her. "How long will you be here?"

32

Harper swallowed against her hurt pride. "At least a week." With Sissy's gloating, she could not admit unemployment, homelessness, and singlehood. Sissy seemed determined tonight to get one better or make her feel small. Harper couldn't bear to let her.

Sissy frowned, peering at her with squinted eyes. "How are you and Clint? The wedding still on?"

Harper's spine stiffened. "Why do you ask?"

"Oh, I just thought that if you were staying here that long, there must be trouble in paradise," Sissy said, tilting her blonde head, pursing her plump lips. Harper's cheeks flared. Always blunt, her cousin ruffled everyone's feathers, and could use some of the etiquette Aunt Effie had always attempted to instill. "I mean, I know Emmett and I are new to the couple department, but I wouldn't want to leave for a week without him. I'd ask him to be here with me."

Choking on the bite she'd swallowed, Harper's eyes watered as the pain stabbed her throat. She managed to get it to slide down with a little sweet tea before responding. "You and Emmett are seeing each other?"

"It was only a matter of time," Sissy said, smiling brightly, her eyes lighting in victory. "We have so much in common. I'm sure you and Clint felt that way when you first started dating."

At six years old, Emmett had been the chubby, freckle-faced boy next door. He'd been so self-conscious, and Sissy had been merciless with her treatment of him, even though he'd been nothing but nice to her. When he'd shot up six inches in seventh grade year and become lithe and lean for track, Sissy had said he was like the frog prince transforming from the toad to the junior high hottie. She'd said this to his face though. In ninth grade, the girls had drooled over him, but he hadn't paid much attention. Sissy made sure his ego never inflated. Emmett had been Harper's best friend and boyfriend, not Sissy's. Sissy would just roll her eyes and say that they needed more drama in their lives.

Something must have changed between the two of them when she'd left.

All of this was long ago though. The past. Who married their childhood sweetheart anyway? When Emmett had been sitting in the kitchen earlier today, she'd seen small pieces of that teenage boy though. The soft, sensitive eyes. The broad shoulders with lean, athletic body. But there had been parts she didn't recognize. A swirl of emotions in his eyes. The strange formal dress.

Harper felt Sissy's gaze burning into her. She shook herself from her reverie, thinking it best she stay away from such thoughts.

"Clint and I are fine."

Grams's fork clanked against the plate. "When will the wedding be, Sweetheart?"

Anxiety trembled through her. She didn't want to lie to her grams, but Sissy waited smugly for an answer. As if she knew she'd failed.

"We were thinking June," Harper said, deciding quickly to go with the original plans and admit the truth later. "Clint wanted a small wedding before the move, but as I look at the details, I don't think that's going to happen."

"Nonsense," Grams said. "Sissy and I can help make it

happen. If that's what you want, of course."

"Why not?" Sissy said, holding her sweet tea glass in one hand and peering at Harper with a look of distrust. "Anything for the golden child."

Grams placed her glass down harshly, her forehead crinkling, her mouth moving to speak.

"Harper," Granddaddy said, "I have a story for you."

"Do you?" Harper said, swallowing her anger as she pulled her glare away from Sissy.

"There's treasure on this property, and me and you are going to find it," He said, excitedly banging his hand against the table. "The Ames treasure is just waiting for us to discover its location."

"You don't say?" Harper said, smiling. Her eyes burned with unshed tears. At childhood sleepovers, this was the same story he'd tell her at bedtime. Her chest ached with the knowledge that the disease had not stolen all the memories from them just yet.

"Yes," he nodded. "In June of 1863, my granddaddy's family got word that the Union and Confederate army would be clashing at Lafourche Crossing, which is in an ear's shot of here."

Granddaddy's eyes lit up with his story. His whole body became animated as he waved his fork in the air in the direction of the train crossing before lowering it to the table to demonstrate the two sides on the white tablecloth.

"Confederate General Taylor had been raiding Union forces, burning plantations, and recapturing liberated slaves, but General Emory for the Union forces couldn't be counted on not to pillage for what they wanted either."

Granddaddy paused and for a moment Harper thought he'd lost the strain of the story, that it had disappeared as well with the chemical synapses. She held her breath, her cheeks aching as she wished with everything for the story to continue.

"My granddaddy's older brother… his name was…" Granddaddy thought for a moment. "Ambrose. His name was Ambrose. He hadn't enlisted as a soldier yet because his mama didn't want him to fight until he was seventeen. He gathered all the family valuables up and made my granddaddy help him."

"What valuables, Granddaddy?" Harper asked, the words scratching the back of her throat. It was her line in this script developed over years of telling.

"Grand-Mère's pearls from France, the silver-plated serving set, jewelry, the gold they'd brought from Europe with them. They gathered it all up and buried it in the back yard without a word to their mother."

"But they didn't draw a map," Sissy said. She and Harper's eyes met. They both seemed to be holding their breath, playing their roles in the story. A momentary truce drawn for their devotion to this man.

Granddaddy chuckled. "No, they didn't, girls. And Ambrose ran off and enlisted after the battle of Lafourche Crossing. Granddaddy thinks he joined before the brigade marched on, but he was only eight years old and he couldn't remember where the treasure was buried once the war was over. He said it was dark and they'd stumbled around a bit, causing him to lose his sense of direction. Ambrose never returned, and it's believed he died in the war not long after enlisting. Grand-Mère didn't want to draw attention to her wealth being missing, so he wasn't to speak of it to anyone."

"But he wrote about it." Harper said, thinking of the well-worn pages of Ellis's journal he'd taken out often to show them. Even with two history degrees and nearly a third, she still hadn't read the book, something she should probably rectify.

"Mmhmm," Granddaddy said, nodding his head. "And that's how we are going to find that treasure."

"No treasure hunting tonight, I'm afraid," Grams said. "Just a nice dinner and a good night's sleep. We can look for the Ames treasure in the morning."

Granddaddy winked at them. "She puts a damper on an adventure, but her cooking makes her worth keeping around, right girls?"

Harper laughed. The conversation was a repeat of so much childhood banter. If she pretended that earlier in the day hadn't happened, everything would be just like it had been back then. Sissy frowned at her from across the table. If she stuck her tongue out at her, it would be even more so.

But, alas, they were too grown up for such actions.

Tears sprang to her eyes as she thought of the morning's events. How she wished she could go back to a time before fifteen, when everything felt simple.

But the complex truth was that her grams had offered to help plan a June wedding that she couldn't go through with because she'd discovered the man she'd lived with for the last six years dallying with her openly gay boss.

The sadness and anger welled inside of her to the point where she knew she must excuse herself.

Emmett

With the door ajar, Emmett gave a cursory knock before entering his father's bedroom without waiting for a response. Besides updated bedding, his father's room had remained virtually untouched since his teenage years. Except for his college years, the man had lived within this room most of his life. A hacking cough vibrated from the floor and the man himself lay curled in a fetal position on the sheepskin rug.

Emmett walked in and stood over him. "Winston."

The dirty mess of clothing groaned, white fur sticking to his lips as he lifted his face from the rug.

Emmett grabbed his father by his thin shoulder blades to help lift him up. "Why are you on the floor?"

"The bed was spinning," he mumbled. "I think it was possessed."

"Maybe it drank too much, too." Emmett's stomach churned from the smell emanating from the man's body, the smell of fermented malt mingled with sweat as it escaped each greasy pore.

"I didn't share," Winston grumbled, stumbling as Emmett

heaved him into the disheveled sheets.

"It's time for a bath."

"C'mon now, don't be like that." He swatted at him, barely grazing his forearm. "I'm just getting started."

Emmett gritted his teeth against further biting commentary while picking up the half empty bottle on the side of the bed. Winston had started a binge eleven days ago. As long as he kept it holed up in this room, Gramps remained quiet. Emmett hadn't mastered the old man's stoic ability to look the other way.

Emmett turned to go, considering bringing a tray of food and leaving it in case he chose to come up long enough to put something besides bourbon inside him. Typically, the average bender lasted fourteen days and he only ate during the peaks.

"Leave the bottle," Winston said, pulling a pillow over his head.

Emmett set it down on the dresser near the door and walked out, rationalizing that there would be others hidden in the room. And at least he wouldn't be driving. Heaven forbid he made that mistake again.

Downstairs, his grandfather had his usual two pieces of toast and scrambled eggs in front of him with his newspaper laid out. His reading glasses rested on the bridge of his nose as he strained to read the tiny print of the court records. Emmett had attempted to introduce him to the online version, but the man had set his habits when the paper had a neighborhood kid tossing it at the door.

"Coffee's in the pot," he said without glancing up.

It must be a good listing today or his eyes were having trouble focusing and he wouldn't admit to it. There was a time that he refused to wear the glasses and claimed his eyesight was 20/20. Any perceived weakness put him at a disadvantage in his view of how the world worked, but with age he'd been willing to make a few concessions.

Emmett noticed his usual mug placed in front of the pot and poured the rich liquid inside, adding a heaping amount of sugar from the small dish to offset the sludge his grandfather had no doubt brewed up.

"When's that interview?" The paper crinkled behind him, announcing the conclusion of the morning read.

Emmett sipped and then cringed. He added another scoop of sugar from the bowl and made a mental note to update the coffee machine to one of those pod things that couldn't be screwed up. His gramps would object at first, but he'd adjust.

Emmett carried his mug to the barstool. "One o'clock."

Gramps raised a bushy white eyebrow. "You have a good suit ironed, correct?"

"Yes sir, it's all pressed. Picked up from the dry cleaners just yesterday."

"You need to make a good impression," he said, picking up a bite of his eggs with his fork. "Not too often people get a second chance."

Emmett sipped his bitter coffee to avoid speaking the many thoughts he had on this matter, all thoughts he'd shared before with the man to no avail.

"I think we need to look into some help for Winston," Emmett said. "Maybe another one of those treatment centers."

"Nonsense," Grandfather said, crunching into his blackened toast. "He made this mess, he needs to lay in it, sleep in it, and he will come up for air with the old Hebert gumption and realize he needs to get back on track."

"I don't think it will be that simple."

"It's not meant to be simple, my boy," Gramps said, waving his piece of toast at him, crumbs splaying across the table. "The road needs to be tough so he doesn't want to go down it again. Just like you having to start all over. You will be much more aware of what's going on around you now, so you don't let it happen to you again."

The burning of the coffee threatened to come up into his esophagus. The conversation and the bad coffee had given him heartburn.

Emmett stood up, unable to tolerate any more of the coffee or conversation. "I'm going to go outside and take some snapshots of Grammy's courtyard. I have a friend who's going to let us know how best to take care of her roses."

"We should get a landscaper to come in," Gramps said. "A professional."

At the kitchen sink, Emmett emptied the contents of the coffee mug down the drain. "Let's see what my friend says. She runs a nursery."

"While you're out there, make sure that imbecile Walter didn't dig holes in the yard. I plan to inspect myself within the hour."

Emmett exited into the mudroom, thinking that the ornery man had only deepened his habits and his inability to change. His plans to ease the man into a life without his wife would be made more difficult by the aging man's own personality.

Harper

Her tummy rumbled beneath the sheets as the warm aroma of drop biscuits wafted in through the cracks in the bedroom door. Harper stirred, pulling the pillow over her head.

Her tummy rumbled louder. She imagined it moved the sheet this time. The exhaustion from that thick sadness plaguing her anchored her to the bed, but the memories of mouth-watering, melt-in-your-mouth biscuits enticed her to toss off the quilt, unable to stand the smell any longer.

She stumbled downstairs pulling a robe tightly around her, wondering how many questions would arise if she refused to get dressed and simply sat outside in the boxer shorts and oversized t-shirt she currently wore. Convincing her family everything was okay might get more difficult, but after a restless night's sleep she didn't care as much as yesterday.

Clint or Filipe had not called since yesterday morning's single attempt. At least one of them could have offered her the opportunity to yell or to hang up or to refuse to listen last night when her brain had begun to process the incident. But neither had called. The idea that they'd spent the night together had made her angry. Six years of her life had revolved around these two men. They'd probably shared a beer and complained about her temper. Perhaps they'd discussed how they'd got one over her for such a long time, congratulating themselves on how smart they were until now. She felt like an idiot, no matter how ridiculous her line of thinking had digressed last night.

"Good morning, Sunshine," Grams said, placing a platter of biscuits on the table by the parlor window. "I wondered when you were going to make an appearance. My biscuits must be losing their touch." She winked at Harper as she returned to retrieve some juice glasses on the counter.

Harper sank into one of the cushioned seats and peered outside, searching for a nice spot to perch herself. That garden bench near the old oak tree looked like a cozy spot. She might have to chase away that chicken pecking at the dirt pathway because she wasn't tempted to share her space today.

"What's with the chickens?" Harper asked, noticing a few of them scattered around the yard.

Grams chuckled as she placed the juice glasses on the table. "Well, your granddaddy decided we needed fresh farm eggs so he bought a dozen chickens. We only have ten left on account of some minor disagreements."

Harper mindlessly picked a biscuit from the heap. "What disagreements?" The biscuit crumbled in her fingers, and she had to cup her other hand under it to avoid morsels falling into her lap.

"Truthfully," Grandmother sighed, sinking into the chair across from her, "he bought the chickens to annoy the Judge. They're noisy and smelly, but to further add to the insult, your granddaddy has decided that they should be free-range chickens for a few hours every morning. Of course, when they freely range onto the Judge's property, I suspect the Judge serves chicken for dinner. I can't confirm that though."

"Oh," Harper said, watching the chickens scuttle around the yard. "*Oh.*"

As she nibbled on the biscuit, she watched as a black chicken scuttled towards the live oaks bordering the Judge's property.

Harper darted toward the back door and shot off after the helpless animal. No chickens were going to be the Judge's dinner on her watch. Recognizing that the two closest men in her life were involved in more than a normal friendship had gone unnoticed and could be all her fault for being completely oblivious to the signs, but she certainly had the skills to save a chicken from a massacre.

The grass was cold and wet beneath her bare feet, and her robe flapped open as she ran through the yard. Her heart pounded with the effort, and her head warned her that this might not be her best idea. The black tale feathers disappearing behind a tree trunk propelled her forward though.

Ducking around the tree, she approached the chicken at a clipped pace, but it hustled faster, darting through the branches of the live oak trees, clucking loudly in its attempts to get away from her. The little bugger was fast. She'd need a different tactic, or she might as well put him in the Judge's pot for him.

Making a wide arch around the trees, she tried to come at it from the front. When she was within inches of its bobbing neck, the chicken clucked and darted toward her left.

"I'm trying to save your life!" Harper yelled, running after it, now completely on the Judge's property, traipsing through the soft, green St. Augustine grass.

A stitch grew in her side as the robe wiped at her legs, but she pushed herself harder. Dumbass—what she'd nicknamed the chicken— stuck his neck out to try and slip away. She dove after it, landing full out on the ground, hands grasped firmly around the body of the chicken.

"Wow," Emmett said, attempting to force down a grin. "I thought you might need some help, but I see you have it covered."

Harper groaned, feeling the sting across parts of her that should not be playing contact sports without protection. "Nothing to see here. Just a chicken rescue."

She sat up, the chicken squirming and clucking in her hands. She didn't want to look at him. This could have been a moment of triumph if she didn't have an audience, especially one who'd known her when she was tough. Right now she wanted to limp away and cry about the pain shooting up her knees.

"I don't think the chicken wanted to be rescued," Emmett said grinning.

Harper struggled to her feet, fighting with the surprisingly strong chicken to keep it in her grasp. "She would if she knew what your grandfather had in store for her."

Emmett's smile faded, and the creases around his eyes softened. "These men must have some kind of record on the longest-standing feud."

Harper began walking back toward her family's property, toward a fenced in cage she supposed was the chicken coop. The shiny aluminum hinted at its newness, and the gate was propped open with a pail. Emmett followed her, lagging a footstep behind.

"It's ridiculous," Harper uttered, hoping she didn't release the chicken with all its squirming. She couldn't handle another chase right now. With all its wiggling and pecking at the air, it must prefer to be free range.

"I agree," Emmett said, nodding. "Perhaps you and I could try and find a way to get them to end it?"

Harper laughed. She released Dumbass into the chicken yard and swung the gate closed. She looked back at the yard and considered how she would get the other nine inside. She didn't suppose chickens came like dogs when called. The only thing she knew about chicken was that Grams could fry it just right.

Emmett swung the door open again. He opened a barrel near the gate and scooped out a shovel full of corn. He tossed it onto the dirt ground. Dumbass immediately began pecking at the corn.

Harper turned and watched as chickens waddled toward them, and as she moved out of the way, they crossed into the gate and began pecking around the chicken coop.

After a brief moment, Harper counted all ten and latched the gate, pulling on it to make sure it stayed closed. No more chicken chasing today.

She glanced at Emmett. His angled jaw appeared clean-shaven and his hair combed into place, but his t-shirt and shorts revealed he hadn't been on his way to work. She'd heard he'd become a lawyer like the rest of his family—she remembered him saying when they were kids that he wasn't going to do that. She realized in that moment looking up at him that she didn't know much about this man, only the boy.

"How did you know to do that?"

"Well," Emmett said sheepishly. "Your grandmother gets me or Sissy to do this for her as soon as your grandfather goes inside to take his bath."

Drats. That would have been a nice piece of information before she made a fool of herself. Maybe if she hadn't run out hell-bent on saving a chicken, Grams could have shared this little trick with her.

Her face burned as Emmett now looked down at her. She could see the laughter lighting up his acorn eyes.

"I hear you and Sissy are an item now," Harper said, adjusting her robe, realizing how much of a mess she must appear. "I was quite surprised, but I'm happy for you two."

Emmett looked taken aback, the unshed mirth disappearing. "Yes, yes, an item."

"And look, I want to try and end the feud, too," Harper swallowed against the surge of emotion that had arisen. It was the happy couple element. Sitting out on her bench, contemplating how happy she'd thought she'd been seemed like a more viable option than talking to a happy couple. "I don't know what good we'll do, but we should try."

"Why Emmett," Grams called from the back porch, "you must come get one of my biscuits. It will get your day started off right."

Harper released a jagged breath. She could see Emmett had remained part of the family. How he'd managed that through the years, Harper couldn't say since she hadn't been around. Maybe he hadn't changed much since those days of treasure hunts in the backyard and games of pretend.

He motioned for her to walk ahead of him. They walked toward the back door, all formal and uncomfortable in silence. They'd changed though. The connection they'd had that had made them feel completely comfortable and like a perfect fit felt like it had never existed.

Emmett

Tapping his fingers against his briefcase, he glanced once more at the paralegal pecking away at the keyboard. Twenty-two minutes had passed since Emmett had checked in with her, and she'd managed to do the impossible and avoid him in the small reception area of the old converted downtown house. The archways and doors still remained from the original floor plan, very much like the building he worked out of until a few weeks ago, a family law firm begun by his great grandfather.

A buzzer emanated from the desk and Stephanie, the paralegal, paused the tapping on the keyboard to reach over and press another button on a large phone.

"I'll see him now," a gruff voice sounded over the speaker.

Emmett stood and waited to be directed toward Brooksy Toups' office.

"It's the last office back there," Stephanie said, peering over her reading glasses. "He usually has his door open."

Emmett nodded and headed down the hall, noticing nameplates on the top of the doors including two he recognized from the courts. Not particularly friendly fellows, he'd never had more than a handshake before a plea agreement or settlement. One door's nameplate was missing, and to his right, the door lay ajar. Brooksy sat behind a massive mahogany desk, his cobalt blue suit and red tie standing out against the neutral beige of the walls and the light oak of the bookcases. A stack of court briefs sat on his desk and he was flipping through a packet as Emmett walked in.

As he approached, Brooksy stood to shake his hand, a firm grip with a squeeze. "I apologize for making you wait. I'm in the middle of a custody battle, and I finally heard back from the judge on the case. I'm sure you know how that works."

Emmett nodded and took the seat across from the desk that Brooksy gestured to with his free hand, his other still holding the documents.

"Thank you for granting me the interview," Emmett said, adjusting his jacket and straightening his favorite orange tie.

"No problem," Brooksy said, his chair creaking as he leaned back in it. "Your grandfather was always good to me. When he called, my interest was piqued since he didn't often ask for favors."

Emmett squirmed, the black pleather cushions not as comfortable as they'd appeared. "After the closing of the family firm, I'm just looking to get back into a practice."

Brooksy's head matched his body—wide football shoulders, still large from his days of walking on to the college team as a freshman. An injury sophomore year had changed his trajectory, but that goal-oriented drive still emanated from his cool eyes. "I've built this firm up with reliable individuals to take on my cases because I'm going into politics. I plan to announce my intentions within the next six months."

Emmett nodded, thinking that's exactly where he could see golden boy back in law school making a name for himself. "I always felt that's where you were heading."

"I'm looking for three lawyers to build our client list while I focus on a campaign. We do have some company law among other litigation. I've hired two individuals in the last eight months, but the last spot has proven a challenge."

"I do have a client list already built from the last few years of practice. Of course, I'd be bringing it with me." Emmett felt his shoulders squaring under the scrutiny. He'd always heard that Brooksy dazzled in the courtroom with his well-groomed dark hair, angular jaw, and a wardrobe outfitted to entertain the cameras instead of judges. But the cool, calculated gaze felt more like an intimidation strategy than a wowing effort. Maybe he'd progressed due to his political aspirations. Emmett wondered exactly what politics he aspired to—was it local, state, or more of a national stage?

Brooksy leaned back and placed his hands together, his fingertips almost grazing his chin. "I'm not looking for any scandals. No fodder for my opponents will be provided because of a favor I owe from fifteen years ago, even for a distinguished man such as your grandfather."

Emmett's pulse quickened. Anger began to curl through him. "I have a clean record in my career."

Brooksy nodded, his head tilting fifteen degrees. "I did make some calls because as I said, my interest was piqued. It's not everyday one gets a call from the great Honorable Judge Hebert."

Emmett sat in the uncomfortable chair and waited, wanting

to hear the words spoken out loud, so he'd know for certain what everyone whispered behind his family's backs.

Brooksy grimaced, the look appalling on his thin lips. "It's your father, isn't it? He became involved in some deals that some are questioning the legality of. It's out there, Emmett, so there's no use pretending it isn't."

Brooksy raised an eyebrow, and still Emmett remained silent, neither denying nor confirming. Neutrality was the best play here. He'd already made his decision about the job, but for the moment, Emmett wanted information.

"I can't bring that into this place," Brooksy said, resting his beefy hands on the shiny polished surface of his desk. "But I tell you what, I believe they are looking for an ADA; I can put a good word in for you."

"Thank you for that." Emmett stood, hearing all he wanted. Brooksy had demonstrated enough class not to gossip, just not enough to refuse to interview him for a job he'd never planned to offer. "Sorry to waste your time."

"I'd be very careful," Brooksy added, leaning back further in his chair, stretching his hands above his head. "Some people may confuse you and your father, and I've heard about some deal that bars him from practicing law again. Any truth in that?"

"About as much truth as there is to any gossip."

Emmett clutched his briefcase containing his hard-wrangled client list and strolled out.

Brooksy had been on a fishing expedition. He'd had no intention of hiring Emmett; he'd taken the meeting to discover exactly why one of the oldest law practices in Thibodaux had closed suddenly. Unlike what he'd admitted to Brooksy, the gossip had come very close to the truth for once.

His father had run their law practice into the ground by taking bribes, offering bribes, and pretty much everything else good lawyers trying to stay on the right side of the law shouldn't do. He'd hired witnesses and paid for evidence to disappear all between alcohol binges. After double crossing a well-known, shady businessman client in the courtroom, he'd become the target of blackmail and then death threats when he hadn't relented. Just when it was to be pubic knowledge, his grandfather had sailed in to clean up the mess. The negotiation had included the sale of the family practice and Winston's clients to a buddy of the Judge who made it all go away, along with an agreement that Winston would stay out of the courtroom—the last part being more for the sake of warding off any future debacles.

This deal also put Emmett out of a job on rather short notice. One day he had an office, and the next morning he'd been told to vacate the premises for the cleaning crew. His grandfather's only comment had been that in the future Emmett should pay attention to what was going on around him more. To soften the blow, he'd added that Emmett was young so he had plenty of time to work hard and do well for himself.

His grandfather was blind when it came to Winston.

Emmett kicked at the tire of his parallel-parked car and considered walking up the streets of Downtown Thibodaux to burn off his frustration. He didn't want to be unemployed. Financially, he'd be fine, but not having something to take action with made him feel listless. If he walked over two blocks though, that would only lead him to the café, and he'd need to have another unwanted conversation with Sissy.

Maybe he just needed to drive, clear his thoughts, and options would come to him.

A middle age, balding man he'd faced in court a few times hustled past clutching a tattered briefcase. His cheeks deepened further into a smile before his neck snapped down so he could stare at his shiny black loafers as he hurried along. No doubt he'd heard something about the Heberts. Probably thought it was Emmett, not his father.

Emmett tossed his briefcase into the passenger seat and sat down in a huff.

Harper

True to her word, Harper spent the day on the bench under the oak tree amongst the ferns. Much to her chagrin, she had changed attire after Grams's insistence. Apparently, her bathrobe would disturb the neighbors. If they were speaking about the Judge, he was already disturbed. Grams didn't typically lose an argument though, and the petite, insistent woman had said that the Judge's questionable sanity wasn't a good enough reason to allow people to see her in nightclothes. Lugging her bag with her dissertation notes and the rejected work in progress towards her selected bench, she'd quelled Grams's questions by assuring the woman that she hadn't lost her mind, but that she would remain outside until she came up with a new topic, so she could complete her degree.

She didn't completely ignore the notes in her bag, but she spent a majority of the hours lolling about in nature or napping sprawled across the quilts she'd also lugged out with her. Having abandoned her cellphone in the bedroom, she figured she'd deal with her thoughts and make a plan for what should come next, without all the outside interference.

By midafternoon the only logical thought she'd strung together was that she needed to start over with her life. She needed a redo. Even her dissertation needed to be scrapped and face a reboot. With fresh eyes, she realized her topic had been just as weak as her professor claimed in his stinging rejection note. She wished she could have seen that clearly before taking all that time off, but then again, she also wished she'd had seen her fiancé was having an affair with her boss before she'd invested all her twenties in the relationship.

Harper flipped the quilt off of her legs and stood and stretched. Maybe a walk would help untangle the cobwebs in her mind and allow solutions to the problems to form.

The Ames family property sprawled on for acres in neatly mowed, endless green grass. Somewhere towards where her line of sight blurred existed a line of trees and the end of Ames' land. The chicken coop had been butted up against an old cypress barn that had probably once been used, but had been in a state of disrepair since Harper could remember. Once she reached the edge of the weathered, rotting wood, a small grove of fruit trees dotted the area. When she'd been young, there had also been a garden—long rows that Granddaddy would till up every spring for Grams to plant. It had been years since Granddaddy had plowed that small patch for her grams. The vegetables had been hit or miss most years, as Grams was more of an experimenter. She'd grown what she felt like eating that season, and sometimes it would just shrivel up as she didn't quite have the knack for it. The fig tree appeared laden with leaves and fruit though, and she'd planted these trees while Harper was growing up. She, Sissy, and Emmett would pull fruit from the branches as they passed by and eat it on the run. It tasted sweeter with the air whipping around them.

Before stepping beyond the citrus grove, Harper steeled herself for the view of her old family home—the one she'd shared with her mother. Her father too, but she didn't think of him when she remembered this house. Fifteen years of neglect would have changed it from what she remembered, she reminded herself. Harper cleared a large grapefruit tree and stopped, startled by the house tucked away at the edge of the property line. She'd expected neglect. Derelict. Crumbling perhaps.

The white picket fence that surrounded the front door area, offering a small eight-by-eight square where her mother used to place a lawn chair to sit out and tan, had a fresh coat of white paint. The flower box on the windowsill had daisies planted in it, and the once yellow house was now a nice shade of Caribbean blue.

"What in the world?" Harper uttered out loud, feeling the smallness of her words around her in the large open area.

No one had lived in this house for fifteen years, but her grandparents had kept the house waiting for someone to come home to it. They'd never mentioned their efforts. Why?

The yellow front door swung open and Sissy emerged, designer bag swinging forward as she hurried through.

Harper felt the moment shatter, a dread creeping in. "What are you doing here?"

Startled, Sissy wiped around, bag swinging. She frowned when she saw Harper. "I can ask you the same question."

Harper jutted her chin out in defiance. "I'm taking a walk."

"Well, I live here," Sissy said, closing the door behind her. "I had to come change my shirt after my incompetent barista spilled the secret sauce all over me." Sissy fidgeted nervously, tugging her blonde hair away from her face.

"You can't live here," Harper said, her brain attempting to process Sissy coming out of her mother's house, a house she'd assumed had sat empty for fifteen years.

"I don't believe you get to decide that fact." Sissy straightened her shoulders, reaching her full 5'8" height. "As I've been living here for two years now, it's a little late for your opinion anyway."

"Two years?" Harper took a step back from her, flabbergasted that no one had bothered to mention it in that long period of time. Sissy must be trying to get under her skin.

Sissy met her eyes. "If you haven't noticed in two years, maybe you should consider how much time you've spent here."

Harper frowned, feeling an anger growing. "This is my mother's house. All her stuff is here."

"Your mother's gone." Sissy crossed her arms across her chest, grimacing at her. "And the house was Great Aunt whoever's house before your mother took hold and made it some thrift store project. Now, I really must get back to work before that insufferable girl burns down my place."

Sissy sailed past her and headed towards her blue '67 Mustang, a gift from her father upon graduation.

Harper studied the house a moment longer, the identical burnt orange flower urns on each side of the door, the decorative throw pillows on the rocker—all of it in color coordinating fabrics. Her mother would have never concerned herself with those details. She would have brought home odds and ends from whatever house she was currently restoring. She'd restored this house using scraps from various jobs and said it gave the house character. There'd been planters derived from old, painted tires. Broken ceramic tile had been reconfigured into beautiful art pieces as well as stepping stones. When she was seven, her mother had returned with a garden gnome family that they'd put by the front steps and given names. Inside had been the quilt Grams had made her parents as a wedding present, old and tattered after so much wash and use, but her mother had allowed her keep it on her bed. There'd been chairs salvaged from the trash and repainted. All projects she'd spent hours helping her mother with, and they'd always end up with paint on them—hair, nose, arms, it didn't matter. They'd have to come clean in that old, cold claw foot tub that Mom said she wanted to change one day, but she didn't have the heart to get rid of the antique one.

Harper found the anger creeping up from her toes and churning through her body at the idea that all of it was gone.

She turned on her heel and marched back toward the main house to find Grams. The woman would have to answer for this.

She found her piecing a quilt in the front room, working with some blue fabric covered with a delicate looking filigree pattern.

Standing over the stooped woman, hand on hip, Harper huffed. "I just took a walk around the property and discovered something that no one thought to tell me in two years."

Grams looked up, her expression blank, the dark circles under her eyes telling. After only her brief stay, Harper suspected the woman wasn't sleeping at night with her worries. Recognition slowly twitched at Grams's lips. "We didn't plan on keeping it secret, Dear. It's just that there never came a right time to bring it up with you. I didn't want to add any more pain."

Harper softened as she saw her Grams's drooping shoulders and misty eyes. "You should have told me."

The old woman's hands trembled as she folded them over the fabric. "A few years ago, you said Clint had no intentions of living here, that he wanted to practice medicine in the city. I figured you weren't coming back. Your granddaddy had taken care of the house all these years for you, but finally he agreed to allow someone else to live in it. Sissy decided it should be her so that she could help out around here."

Harper didn't remember having this conversation with her grams. It was true that Clint hoped for an appointment at a big city hospital. He dreamed of a busy floor and a hectic schedule, but Harper had always assumed that one day, life would lead her back here somehow. Sacrificing for a few years had been manageable, but she figured Clint would have to return the favor later. Maybe she'd deceived herself, though, as she'd not seen other issues that should have been glaringly obvious. It was true that Clint would find an excuse not to come visit her family. Claiming exhaustion from his work schedule had seemed reasonable at the time, but now in light of new events maybe he had other motives.

It was so frustrating to question every choice she'd made the last six years.

Harper focused on the woman in front of her to distract herself from the self-loathing. "All my mother's belongings were in that house."

"We packed some of them up and moved them into the attic for you."

Grams looked at her, waiting for her to say it was okay, to offer her forgiveness.

"Someone should have told me."

Harper could have been speaking to numerous people with this statement. But a little voice in her head argued that she'd not paid attention. She should have noticed all of this—all of the things going wrong in her life.

Emmett

Emmett fiddled with the empty soda fountain glass sitting on the glassy tile counter. The Bittersweet Café stayed open until 7:00 two nights a week, and the little sandwich shop had found a regular crowd even though Sissy had initially tried it as an experiment. The afternoon special revolved around a root beer float that Emmett was partial to after having grown up slurping them down on Mrs. Ames's back porch. Now, the recipe was considered top secret and only available during the afternoon "dessert hour," even to him.

Sissy weaved around the four remaining tables in the small area, picking up the sandwich baskets and chatting with the regulars. It was in this place that she seemed to relax and release the high strung Sissy he'd known all his life. All the skepticism he'd had about Sissy serving people had evaporated as he'd watched her work that first time. She'd found her calling, unlike himself, who couldn't even find a job.

After driving for two hours, he'd released the anger. With the windows rolled down, the tie tossed in the back seat, the first two buttons undone, and the sleeves rolled up, he'd let the frustration and disappointment blow away. He didn't know what the answer to his future was yet, but he wouldn't be relying on his grandfather's connections to figure it out. He needed to work his career out on his own. Even after driving enough to reach this conclusion, though, he still wasn't ready to break the news to his grandfather.

The man would have one of two reactions. One possibility would be that he'd blame Emmett; say that he simply blew the interview and was only imagining the direction of the conversation. Emmett's newly found calmness wasn't ready to be tested with that reaction. The other possibility would be that he'd realize that his good name had been ruined. Finally, the man who'd staked his life and career on his reputation would have to face the fact that he hadn't covered it up as well as he thought, and people didn't want to believe in his righteousness anymore. Emmett didn't want to be the one to deliver that blow to the man's admittedly overinflated ego.

So, he'd come to Bittersweet for reinforcements in the form of a root beer float and a pep talk.

Sissy didn't seem in the mood for the latter.

She returned behind the counter and began tossing trash and returning baskets under the counter in fluid, hurried movements.

"I just can't believe she expected no one to live in that house," Sissy fumed. "It's not like I wanted to give up my great apartment two years ago. It was downtown and spacious and within walking distance of this place, like upstairs to be exact. But no, my father and uncle thought someone needed to be close to the grandparents to look after things, and who else could they guilt trip? All the other cousins are married or in school or living in the city unconcerned with anything going on around here, like Ms. Harper. If I would have been married or engaged, they would have left me alone too, I bet." She glanced up at him from her cleaning, and he straightened up, knowing it was his turn.

"You like that house though, and the rent is great."

"Is it though?" Sissy said, her eyes piercing through him. She and Harper had similar expressive eyes, but Sissy's green was muddled with more yellow. "It's not really free if I'm always making sure the groceries are stocked and the nurse visits every week and they make it to all their doctor's appointments. I tell you, my father and uncle knew what they were doing. They get to go about their lives without paying for someone to care for them or having to do it themselves."

Emmett nodded, understanding that she wanted his agreement and nothing more.

"And I'm always here for everything, but what do they always comment? If only Harper would be here," Sissy continued, vigorously wiping down the counter she'd already cleaned. "She stayed away for eight years before she came for a first visit. Walked right in as if she'd never been gone. Do you know how much changes in that amount of time? And no one thinks maybe that fact should take away some of that shine they seem to always see when they look at her."

"I'm sure it was difficult for her to return here after her mother's death."

Sissy paused in her scrubbing to glare at him. "Don't do that. Don't make excuses for her. It's enough that everyone else does it."

"You know," Emmett said, feeling like he did growing up when he mediated between the two. In fact, Harper being home had stirred up many old feelings. "Harper mentioned that we are seeing each other. Know anything about that?"

Sissy's shoulders sagged as her eyes dropped to the counter. "Well, we had that one date and there was that wedding we attended that we could count as a second."

Emmett strummed his fingers on the counter as he looked at her and waited for her to look at him.

"Oh, all right," she said, meeting his gaze and offering him a half smile. "I just didn't want to feel like I was coming up short. I always feel like I'm losing against her."

"No one's losing, Sissy. It's not a competition."

"That's where you're wrong." Sissy winked at him as she walked around the counter toward a signaling customer.

Feeling no more motivation to return home than when he'd arrived at the cafe, he did have an additional item to add to his thought deliberations, and at least this one didn't involve dwelling on his own miserable predicament.

Since he'd seen Harper at the Ames home, he hadn't been able to stop thinking about the fun, adventurous girl she'd been. The skinny girl that had been as tough as any boy, always willing to climb a tree and get a skinned knee had grown into a beautiful woman. All the good memories he had of their actually being a couple at fourteen and fifteen had been drowned by the last time he'd seen her though. In her ranting, Sissy was wrong about at least one thing. Harper had returned home in that eight-year span.

Thirteen months after she'd left, she'd arrived spitting rain and tears at his back door. Ranting and cursing him and his family, she'd been animalistic in her blame of him for covering up her mother's death. They'd been sixteen by then. In the year she'd been gone, he'd thrown himself into football, a sport he'd never played before, but it distracted him from the loss of his best friend. He'd changed, grown hard towards his family. He'd barely spoken to them even when in the same room. The house had become an uncomfortable tomb for the walking dead, no one really living inside.

Emmett had been unaware until that night what his grandfather had done, what deals he'd made behind chamber doors. He'd confronted the weary, pale-faced, trembling man after Mr. Walter had dragged Harper from their back courtyard still cursing the Hebert name. Emmett's grandfather had pled with him to understand that Winston needed their help, that he'd only done what he needed to do to help his son. Emmett had felt sick, but he didn't have any words that would make the pain ripping through Harper go away.

Sissy must not know about this visit. Why they would have kept it a secret, he didn't know. At that time, he wasn't allowed to speak to the family because of the impending trial. Emmett's father had killed Harper's mother. A drunk driving accident.

But then there was a plea deal with probation instead of any actual punishment.

How Harper had learned the details from Pennsylvania, he didn't know.

But the image of her soaking wet from the rain, hair sticking to her face, and her chin and lips screwed up in pain as she spit curses at him would never leave his memory.

Sissy hadn't seen that. If she had, she might understand why Harper had not returned for all those years.

Back then, even after a year, he'd been pining for her, thinking that one day she'd return to him, and they would continue where they had left off. But he'd seen it all end that night. Their childhood love had been snapped in half and broken like that tree that had finally stopped his father's Challenger the night he'd killed Beth Ames.

Harper

When she reached for her phone on the nightstand to check the time, it alerted her to fourteen voice mails. Her empty stomach lurched. Someone had gone to the extra trouble of leaving a message instead of hanging up like normal people did these days. She'd need coffee and a biscuit inside to quell the nausea before she dealt with that kind of eagerness in the morning.

Snapping her robe shut, she went in search of breakfast, leaving the offending device on the nightstand. Downstairs, her grams had the biscuits covered and the coffee already brewed. The woman sat in a well-placed rocker glancing repeatedly out of the back windows. As Harper watched, her nimble fingers felt their way over delicate stitch work on a square.

"I hope you had a peaceful night's sleep," Grams said without glancing her way.

"I did." Harper poured coffee into a mug. She couldn't remember having any disturbing dreams to keep her dwelling on anything she wished to avoid. Progress. "I think I'm going to spend the day with Granddaddy and see what stories he can tell."

"Then you might need a shovel, Sweetheart," Grams said,

nodding toward the window. "Today is a digging day."

Harper sipped on the coffee as the woman's soft-spoken words sunk in. Realizing that Grams usually quilted in the front room where all her containers of fabric were neatly stacked, Harper strolled toward the window to see what was going on.

Out the window, about four feet over the left of the property line, her granddaddy leaned over a shovel wiping his forehead with a handkerchief.

"Why are you letting him dig? Shouldn't we try and stop him?" Harper asked, an edge in her voice. Yesterday, he'd sat in his recliner not speaking much. She didn't see how he had the energy for this today or how it could be a good idea for them to let him expend his energy on something so physical.

Grams sighed. "Today is a good day. He's up. He's got purpose, so it's difficult to tell him that what he's doing is wrong."

Harper sipped her coffee silently, considering how difficult this predicament was. The sadness weighed heavily in the creases of her Grams's face. The woman was strong, but the cracks were beginning to show from the stress.

Harper swallowed against the emotion. "So, he's having a good day today?"

"Oh, yes," Grams said, looking up at her with a smile. "He woke up to the smell of biscuits and a plan in place. I think it's one he worked out a few nights ago, but of course he remembers working it out last night."

Overwhelming sadness swallowed Harper for a moment as she watched her granddaddy get back to shoveling. This man had filled her bedtime stories with tales of the treasure and how it could be found. When she'd questioned him about his plans to search for it, he'd always told her he would wait until she grew up to help him, that two Ames minds were better than one. She'd waited too late to aid him with this task though. She didn't see how he'd discover it in his health.

She watched him consult a drawing and scratch his head. "How often does he have good days?"

"When they can get the medication to work, they come pretty often. They've been playing with the dosage though, and the bad days have been too numerous. I'm sure they will get it right soon."

Harper frowned. Maybe someone else needed to speak to the doctor. Uncle Richard lived in town with his wife, and Uncle Phillip in Shreveport was supposed to have been consulted as well. She'd been told the two sons would stay on top of things. She'd assumed staying on top of it meant the doctor's appointments.

Grams looked up at her, resting her stitch work in her lap. "I do hope everything will be okay with you spending all this time here. I'm sure Clint misses you. We don't mind if you invite him here."

Harper thought about the missed calls and wondered if Clint had missed her, had perhaps regretted his choices. But then anger burned her ears at even entertaining the idea of sympathy for the man who could betray her so easily.

"Clint's really busy with work right now," Harper said, trying to keep the edge out of her voice, realizing it still slipped in. "I think I'm going to help Granddaddy."

"There's a pair of boots in the upstairs closet," she said.

"Knowing him, you will be shoveling, so go out there prepared."

Harper laughed, heading back upstairs to change. They may never find the Ames heirlooms, but she could certainly use some time with her granddaddy. Perhaps he could spark some of that old, adventurous Harper that must still dwindle in the ashes of this mess she'd made of her life.

Emmett

Emmett entered the kitchen just as his grandfather slipped a shotgun shell into the old 22 Winchester that the man had received one Christmas when he was a boy. Stopping in his tracks, Emmett's thoughts immediately traveled to yesterday and how his stoic stance must have been a façade. Contrary to Emmett's expectations, his grandfather remained silent when Emmett had delivered the news about the job interview. Emmett had been uncertain how to take it, but he'd figured a reaction would come after the initial shock wore off.

He hadn't expected this though.

Cautiously, Emmett approached the table. "What's going on?"

"I've had it with that man."

Emmett rested his hands on the chair. "Look, I know Winston has been a handful lately, but I don't think this is the best way to handle him."

"Don't be ridiculous," his grandfather said, snapping the barrel in place. "I'm talking about Walter Ames, the man you obviously didn't do a good job of warning to stay off my property. I gave him a civilized warning, but apparently, he needs something else."

Emmett inhaled painfully from his strained lungs. "Gramps, this isn't a good idea. You may mean to scare him, but something could go horribly wrong."

"Who's trying to scare someone?" Gramps said, clutching his shotgun as he walked toward the back mudroom door.

Emmett walked after him, his mind racing over various scenarios, none of them ending well. "Gramps, you need to listen to reason. This feud has gone far enough. The man is ill. He may not even remember who you are if it's a bad day."

"Pitiful excuses," Gramps said, walking at a clipped pace. "Be careful boy, you're sounding like an Ames."

"No, I'm sounding like someone who is trying to stop an old man from spending the rest of his days in prison."

"I have too many connections for that, besides I'd be doing everyone a favor. The man is a nuisance."

Chasing after his gramps, Emmett realized how good of shape his grandfather remained in. Must be the daily exercise he insisted upon. The man still lifted weights at his age and worked out on the machines to keep his heart healthy.

Once outside, Emmett could see Mr. Walter holding a water bottle and Harper, hair tied back, shoveling dirt from a growing hole. He couldn't help feeling an attraction to her even though she was adorned in swamp boots and tattered jeans. She must have been keeping herself in shape somehow as well. He alone must be spending too much time behind a desk—or had been anyway. He didn't have any excuse to be out of shape now, he supposed.

His grandfather raised the rifle to chest level, and the adrenaline began pumping through Emmett. This was not going to end well.

Harper

Harper leaned on the shovel a moment, the blisters on her palms throbbing against the wooden handle. Since she didn't do anything more strenuous with her hands these days than ice a cupcake, she couldn't expect anything but her hands to be rubbed raw. As a child her hands were heavily calloused from shovels and dirt and rocks and rope. All her schooling had made her soft.

"Up until the 1920s, there was a tractor shed here," Grandfather said, puzzling over a drawing. "When the Ames family got out of the family business, it was torn down so the land could be sectioned off."

"Right," Harper said, sinking the shovel into the dirt, two worms squirming to the surface. "Is that when the family went into antiques?"

"Certainly." Grandfather nodded, stepping out of what she assumed was the old shed. "My father had no luck farming, said he didn't inherit a green thumb. Boy, am I glad he chose a different family business." He chuckled.

He was in such good humor. Grams was right. Trying to

discourage him seemed a heartless endeavor. He had too much passion and energy and memory to shut him down.

As the dirt piled up and the holes grew greater, the old expression "a needle in a haystack" came to mind. "So how did you pick this location?"

He came stand by her and examine the deep recesses of the holes. "From the details I've gathered, I believe it's near a structure on the property. I've already dug around the ones that still exist."

Harper nodded, thinking of all the structures that had existed in the time the Ames family had owned the property. She had no idea how many that might be. "So now you've moved onto the ones that aren't there anymore."

Granddaddy grinned. "Of course, logical next step."

The rustling of tree branches caught Harper's attention, and she glanced behind her to see Judge Franklin Hebert coming toward them with a shotgun pointing in their direction. Instinctively, Harper moved in front of her grandfather.

"What are you doing?"

The Judge's lips curled into a gnarled grimace. "Lady, that's a fine question coming from someone who is destroying my neat lawn."

"We aren't destroying anything." Harper huffed, gripping the shovel, considering its possibilities to defend against the rifle. "We will refill the holes, and since it's spring, the grass will grow back within two weeks."

"Not good enough," he replied, raising the barrel. "You are trespassing."

"Gramps." Emmett emerged from behind, out of breath. "That's enough."

"Your gramps needs to lower the weapon," Harper muttered.

"I don't let the kid do my dirty work," the Judge said, keeping the gun level. He'd fired many a rounds hunting rabbits in the back field. Harper did not doubt that his aim was true.

Granddaddy waved his arm out, clutching the map. "All this property is Ames property on the map I have. I think that always angered you."

The Judge stepped closer, shotgun between them. "It's Hebert property on all the maps that count."

Granddaddy stepped out from behind her, even though she attempted to edge him back with her arm. "In everyone's mind this will always be Ames land. That really burns your hide, old man. Just admit it so we can move on."

"That's rich coming from you." The Judge yanked the butt of the rifle up. "I believe you're the one who needs to move on from the past."

Gramps lunged forward. Harper caught him with her arm because he wasn't as quick as he once was, and his knee didn't quite hold the weight he put forward.

The Judge sneered. "What's the matter? You can't handle the truth?"

"You, sir, are a bully," Harper said, squaring her shoulders. "Nothing more than a schoolyard bully who misuses his power to get what he wants."

The Judge sneered at her, but she stood her ground, unblinking under his scrutiny. Most men twice her age were intimidated by him, but she refused to cower.

"And I'm sure you are aware that you can't build anything ten feet from your property line by law," Harper fumed. "So I don't much see a good defense for doing anything illegal with that shotgun for only four feet of your property."

Emmett's hands were on his hips, and he appeared uncomfortable. "She's right, Gramps. Let's go back inside and let them fill the holes."

The Judge glared at them before finally lowering his shotgun.

"What is going on out here?" Sissy approached from the back all made up for the day, heels sinking into the grass.

The Judge yanked his head towards the Ames house. "Your entire family is crazy, Sissy. Get out while you can." He glared at Emmett. "*You*, you can stay here and supervise that every speck of dirt goes back to fill those holes." He waved his finger at Granddaddy. "One more time old man, and I'm going to have you locked up."

He turned and stormed back toward the house.

"I'm really sorry," Emmett said, shaking his head. "I tried to stop him, but he's determined to cause trouble."

"No need," Sissy said. "I can't believe Grams let Granddaddy dig again. I just spoke to her about this. And you," She pivoted and glared at Harper. "How could you be helping him? You have to see it's not our property."

"Give her a break," Emmett said, winking at Harper. "It's only four feet. No harm done."

"I don't call the shotgun waving a safe activity," Sissy admonished, her hands on the hips of her black pencil skirt.

"Nonsense," Granddaddy said, flapping the map in the air. "Treasure hunting isn't supposed to be safe."

Harper looked around at the six holes they'd dug this morning to no avail. Granddaddy wasn't going to find a treasure this way, if the treasure even still existed on the property. It was all random and chance. She could be three inches over from where it was buried and have missed it. But if digging kept him moving around and remembering, she could see how it should be allowed to continue. If only they could get the nasty feud to end, so it was also safe.

Harper looked at Emmett. "I guess you've had no luck on your side ending this feud?"

"I'm working on it," Emmett said, shaking his head. "It would be easier if the man wasn't so stubbornly in denial."

"Ah," Granddaddy said. "The man has always been like a mule. You have to kick him to get him to change directions."

Emmett laughed.

Harper could see Sissy looking disgruntled over something. The girl had certainly grown up to be prissier than she was as a child, if that was possible. But even more than that, she seemed personally affronted by Harper, and Harper didn't understand why.

"Some of us have to get to work," Sissy said, glancing Harper's way. "You need to clean up this mess. We have to live here after you go home to Clint."

"Or perhaps Clint and I should move here, and then we can make a mess until we find that treasure."

Harper didn't know why she said it because there certainly wouldn't be a "Clint and I" in this or any scenario, but the superiority complex that Sissy had developed had grown annoying. Harper didn't remember her being so awful when they were children. Or perhaps as children they'd looked past such slights.

Sissy raised her eyebrows. "Wouldn't that be great?"

She strolled off toward her car, leaving them standing together.

Emmett grinned. "Have another shovel?"

Part II

Harper

Coming downstairs, Harper heard voices within the house when she turned the corner of the banister. This could be a good sign. Hoping Granddaddy was having a good day, she'd made plans to take him down to the antique store. For the last sixty years of his life, he'd spent most Saturdays toiling around the shop, polishing and cleaning up inventory while customers milled around. She'd woken up and thought it would be a good day to revisit his old place, maybe recapture memories that were slipping away.

Entering the front room, she found Grams and Sissy sitting on the old Victorian settee with their heads bent together.

"What's going on?" Harper asked, scanning the room for Granddaddy and coming up empty. "I'm hoping to take Granddaddy out today."

Sissy waved her hand in the air as if pushing the thought away. "Have a seat. Grams and I have something to discuss with you."

Harper didn't like the saccharine drip in her voice. Unless an angel had visited the snippy woman last night to show her the consequences of her wicked ways, something was up.

Sitting in the Queen Anne chair, Harper waited, her suspicions in overdrive.

"So Grams and I had a conversation last night," Sissy said, straightening out the slight wrinkle in her abstract flower skirt. "We've decided to throw you and Clint an engagement party here at the house."

Harper leaned back in the chair, relieved that Sissy hadn't conspired to cause trouble. A party she could wiggle out of with an excuse didn't seem bad. "Oh, that's not necessary."

Grams beamed, tapping her fingers together lightly. "We want to, Sweetheart. It would be a joyful reason to get the family together, perhaps one last time." A slight flicker in Grams's eyes revealed the hidden emotion behind her words.

"Yes." Sissy nodded. "And of course we can invite all your old friends as well as your new friends from the city. You won't have to do anything if that's what has you worried. I know you were never one for these sorts of things."

A panic crept into Harper's chest as she realized how committed they were to the idea. She needed to get out of this. She could admit the truth, but Sissy staring smugly across from her prevented the words reaching above that large ball of pride in her throat. "Maybe Clint and I should decide on a wedding date first. His work schedule may delay it so much that we should wait for a long time."

"That's the best part." Sissy squealed, glancing down at her coordinating wristwatch.

Harper's heart beat harder against her chest. The earlier relief she'd felt had long disappeared. Sissy had planned something.

The doorbell rang, echoing throughout the rooms of the home.

"Right on time," Sissy said, springing to her feet, her flower dress bouncing around her.

"Who?" Harper asked, watching Sissy bounce out the room. Her cousin was much too chipper. Something terrible must be in the works.

"Sissy worked all of this out yesterday." Grams smiled, patting her hair as if one strand of hair would be out of place in her coif. "When that girl gets an idea into her head, she can't be stopped."

Harper swallowed against the terror building. It was clear that Sissy didn't have a change of heart in one night and decide to make Harper's life better. The woman had an ulterior motive. Harper only hoped for a party planner behind that door, one that she could easily dispense.

Listening intently to what was happening at the entrance, Harper heard a distinctly familiar male voice and shot up from the chair, a violent tremble overtaking her.

As she stood there struggling with the desire to bolt, Sissy strolled into the room with Clint two footsteps behind her.

"Harper, we will have no problems scheduling," Sissy said, her smile too wide. "Clint has come to help with the planning."

"How…how," Harper stuttered, trying to catch her breath. Seeing him in front of her caused so many emotions to rise up. She felt light-headed. "How did this happen?"

Clint crossed over to her, and Harper shrunk back from his approaching touch. "Sissy called me last night and revealed her fantastic plan, and I knew it was time to come and help out over here."

Forcefully pulling away from the hug he'd pulled her into,

she took several steps back from him. She fiddled with her shaking hands in the front of her chest to add to the space between them. "What about work?" She'd tried for a breezy airiness to her voice, but the dryness in her throat made it sound like a croak instead.

"In two weeks I have a fellowship interview, but right now I have an exam to study for, and that can be done from anywhere. I'll drive to the city for my last few shifts when it's time." His smile twitched, and fear clouded his eyes. He waited with bated breath for her reaction.

He'd depended on her not calling him out on anything in front of her family. He'd taken a risk, something he didn't typically do.

"Isn't it fantastic, Harper?" Sissy said, clasping her hands together. "We can have the party in two weeks, and Clint will be here to help with all the decisions."

Harper glanced toward Sissy and wondered what the woman was getting out of this. She didn't get her panties in a bunch unless it served her purposes. Had she discovered something about Clint and her, and this was simply an attempt to embarrass Harper?

Harper needed to get a handle on this mess. "Clint, why don't you and I speak privately on the back porch for a second?" Harper needed him to return to New Orleans, and then she could explain to Grams in private. She didn't know where she'd go with it from there, but it was a start. There were still those pesky details about where to live and work now that she'd lost both in one moment, but she needed to begin moving forward.

"Right now, Harper?" Sissy whined. "We have so much to

do! We should get started right away."

Harper wanted to throttle that woman. It wouldn't take much with that scrawny neck of hers.

"We could talk later?" Clint said, hope dripping in every enunciated syllable.

"No," Harper said, dragging him along by his wrist, not wanting the touch of his hand in hers. "Best if we get it out of the way."

She glanced back and offered a plastered smile to Grams's perceptive expression. The woman wasn't a fool, but Harper would deal with problem one before taking on problem two.

Outside, she paused on the porch, but then thought of paper-thin walls and cracks in doors and all the spying she'd done as a child, and she marched him toward the chickens.

"Oh, gross," Clint said repulsed, stopping near the old crabapple tree. "I didn't know the place had turned into a farm."

Harper glared at him, deciding to let his pretentious, city-boy comment slide. "What are you doing here?"

"I'm so sorry, Harper," Clint said, turning his deep blue pleading eyes on her. "I tried calling a dozen times yesterday, but you wouldn't pick up, and I didn't know where you were. I was worried that you'd…" He shuddered. "I swear to you, it didn't mean anything. I made a huge mistake. I was under so much stress, and you know how Felipe is. I don't even know how it happened. I mean, I'm not gay…" His eyes grew wide, and he ran his fingers through his sandy brown hair. "I've never been so sorry."

Harper gritted her teeth together. "How long?"

Clint fidgeted with his ear. "What?"

Harper tapped her foot against the grass. "How long has this been going on between you two?"

"Only a couple of weeks," Clint reached out and grabbed her hands. "But I promise you it's over."

"You're right," Harper said, pulling her hands away, his touch feeling strange. "It's over."

He attempted to reach out and touch her again. "Give me another chance to prove myself to you. Since I saw you standing in that doorway, you are all I can think about. I'm sick with guilt."

"I can't trust you," Harper said, crossing her arms across her chest. "You and Felipe have been friends since you were five years old."

Clint's lips straightened and he studied her. "Then why haven't you told your family?"

Harper stepped back. "I plan to. I was just waiting for the right time."

"Then give me a few days," he begged. "Let me prove to you that you can trust me. If you decide you still want to end things, then I'll leave quietly."

"Are you crazy?" Harper asked, a shrill-pitch tone she didn't like entering her voice. She was losing control of her emotions. "I just caught you cheating on me with a man. It's going to take more than a few days."

"Then let's go inside and tell them that there will be no party."

Harper remained quiet, her mind racing. This was not how she had planned to break the news to her grams, especially with Clint in the room. Grams would be disappointed in her for not revealing the truth earlier.

"That's what I thought," Clint said, putting a hand on his hip and wrinkling his jacket. "How about I help you pretend everything is going great between us, and you agree to give me a second chance."

Harper glared at him. Could the man be more insufferable?

Emmett

Studying the wilted flower petals and crumbling dried leaves, Emmett contemplated all the gardening advice he'd received in under thirty minutes and told himself yet again that he should have written the instructions down. His overconfidence at the time and his unwillingness to look like an idiot in front of his friend's girlfriend had prevented such necessities.

Eleanor, Ellie for short, had rambled on about his grandmother's Tea Roses, continually referring to them as Mrs. B.R. Cant, and talking about how Mrs. B.R. Cant needed a mild pruning, but not too much or it would damage them as it was spring. She'd shown him how to deadhead the sagging, browning mess- a term he'd previously only used for the guys he'd considered losers with no ambition in life. Men like his father and several guys in high school who'd smoked weed and decided against any type of steady job.

These little buggers had thorns though, and his grandmother's tiny gloves wouldn't fit on a man's hands. Besides, he couldn't bring himself to move the flowered pair from her clipping basket where she'd placed them, expecting to use them her next gardening day. They waited expectantly still, uncertain why they'd gone so long between uses when they never had before.

He still had Noisette Roses on the trellis at the entrance of the courtyard to handle, and Ellie had rattled on about whatever kind of bushes were bordering the far side of the patio. Maybe hiring a landscaper shouldn't be out of the question, but the spendthrift judge would only spend the money on such an activity once; therefore, he'd order a landscaper to chop every drop of green growth down.

Emmett wouldn't take the risk of losing this last piece of his grandmother.

"Waste of time, if you ask me," Winston said. In shorts and a ratty gray t-shirt, Winston stretched himself out against a wooden chaise lawn chair sunning himself. He looked terrible with his greasy hair, scruffy beard, and bloodshot eyes covered by dark sunglasses.

Emmett frowned. "No one asked you."

"Hey," Winston said, chuckling. "I'm just trying to make conversation."

"Why?" Emmett said, snipping it at an angle, five leaves down as Ellie had shown him. He watched as it tumbled and fell among the other dead foliage. "Why have you come down from your room?"

Winston tapped on the wooden armrest, disturbing the quiet air. "I can't stand the smell anymore; it was making me nauseous."

Emmett glanced over and saw a glass jug in his hand with clear liquid inside. Perhaps he'd decided to detox. It was a vicious cycle of binges and detoxing, but he showed no sign of wanting it to end. This morning when Emmett had passed his bedroom door on the way to the bathroom, there was a distinct odor emanating from the ajar door. He'd hurried past to avoid inhaling the body odor, stale alcohol, and cigarette smoke.

"It will still smell," Emmett said, motioning with the clippers toward the cigarette dangling from Winston's fingers.

"Nah," Winston said, inhaling a drag. "I have that housekeeper, that Hispanic woman that the old man likes, cleaning up right now."

"You're disgusting," Emmett said, snipping at another wilted rose. It was abuse to have someone clean up after him.

"Didn't mean to offend." Winston chuckled. "Hey, isn't that the girl from next door? The one you couldn't stop following around like a lap dog as a kid?"

Reflexively, Emmett turned toward the Ames house and saw Harper standing near the chicken coop speaking to Clint, a man he recognized from the one time he'd met him at an Ames barbeque. Looking all worked up, her face held some of the unbidden emotion he'd known in their youth, not the reserved poker face he'd witnessed the last few days.

"If you mean Harper Ames, then yes," Emmett said, returning his gaze to the roses, but feeling drawn to the scene unfolding just shy of the tree line. The shrubbery and clucking chickens absorbed their voices, so he could only see a heated discussion unfolding.

"I guess you missed your chance," Winston said, tapping his water bottle again. "I think I did you a favor with that one though. She looks like a handful."

Favor? A revulsion rose like fire up his esophagus. Emmett took four steps towards his father before he stopped himself. The man wanted a reaction. He'd only be giving him what he wanted... what he deserved too, but still.

Winston chuckled. "Relax. Don't be so serious all the time. If you want her that badly, I'm sure there's still time. Her mom was a firecracker, nothing like you'd expect from that stuffy family. Pretty face, but she had these rough hands that were always stained ugly."

"She worked with her hands." The words wouldn't rise above the lump in his throat. Suddenly, he was sweating. Winston spoke so nonchalantly, as if he was the one with dementia and had forgotten he'd killed the woman.

"Right." Winston grunted. "Didn't she repair old houses or some crazy shit like that? Who would have thought a woman like her would do something like that? I guess that's what happens when your husband leaves you."

Emmett snapped at two roses in a row, not paying attention to what he was doing. "She was doing that long before she married Curtis."

"Probably why he left then," Winston said. "No one wants a woman with such rough hands to touch him."

"Right, Winston." Emmett grumbled. "I heard you tried to date her, but she didn't want anything to do with you."

Silence greeted his retort, and Emmett gradually slowed down the rate he clipped the roses. Between the Judge and Winston, he may be the sane one now, but if he had to deal with them too long, that may not remain true for long.

"I think you're too late on that one though," Winston said.

Emmett glanced in Harper's direction and could see the two walking back toward the big house. Harper appeared agitated, temple furrowed. Clint, meanwhile, looked about himself smiling. He wondered what was going on between the two. He wouldn't pretend that his interest hadn't been piqued by her return, but he found it difficult to muster any hope in her regards. Since fifteen, he'd had to be practical about life, and life did not give you back childhood things like innocence, trust, or love.

"Why don't you do something useful, Winston?" Emmett said, snapping angrily with the sheers.

"I am, Son." Winston chuckled. "I am."

Harper

Pushing back against a rack of tea length numbers that even her mother would have difficulty repurposing, she hoped the racks wouldn't close in on her and bury her until the dresses came back in style. The distinct smell of mothballs and sealed up, stale air took her back to Great Aunt Rosie's huge closet in that narrow hall that she and Sissy would hide in while Grams enjoyed coffee and gossip with her sister downstairs.

Harper bumped against a rack of frumpy, potato sack-looking dresses as she attempted to move toward Sissy. "Sissy, I need to get out of this place."

Sissy glared at her from where she stood, holding a dress at arm's length. "You haven't found a dress yet."

Harper scanned the racks from her location. "I will wear something I have in my closet."

She wouldn't need a dress because this party would never happen. As Sissy shopped, Harper considered her options for withdrawing gracefully. She figured she could speak to Grams alone. A classy lady, the woman would know how to wiggle out of this party tactfully, hopefully without making a big announcement.

Sissy hung the dress back on the rack and huffed as she stared her down. "Harper, I took off of work today to get things done for this party. Don't waste my time, please. Clint said you needed a dress."

"I have plenty of dresses," Harper muttered. Not that Clint would have noticed. They hadn't had time to socialize with his residency hours at the hospital and his studying for his last round of licensing exams. She sat through every agonizing conversation as he debated a specialty, worried about his residency appointment, and studied for each stage of the licensing exams, but he couldn't once take her to a museum or a party. Takeout food was his specialty.

Sissy peered at her over her nose. "Are we even related? A party is a great reason to get something new."

Harper thought about the money in her bank account. It wouldn't last long if she didn't go to a job everyday. Of course, she wouldn't be spending the money she'd saved for that wedding dress, but she wouldn't be wasting it on a party dress either.

Sissy pulled out a blue number from the folds of the rack. "This color would look good on you, perhaps. I mean, I don't know about this flower print on your hips, but you should try it on."

"Why don't you try it on," Harper said, weaving her way out of the racks, "while I get some air for a moment."

"Ooh," Sissy said, grabbing another dress from the rack, a light yellow smock. "I'll find some options for you to try on. I'd say a size 6 with those hips, maybe?"

Harper gritted her teeth together and found the door of the consignment store.

"Harper?"

She walked out with Sissy still calling after her. The anorexic twig could figure it out herself. Harper's tolerance threshold had decreased from childhood.

Outside, the air felt better, even if the smell of exhaust and oil marred the freshness of the spring day. Downtown buildings involved parallel parking and uneven sidewalks, but the brick structures with shutters and French provincial lighting fixtures still held its charm. The consignment shop was only a block from the antique store. Contemplating taking a walk over, she figured Sissy wouldn't miss her for at least fifteen minutes as she waded through that mess. Harper didn't believe the sophisticated clothes the woman wore came from anywhere but a department store, no matter what she had insisted when they had arrived.

The downtown streets didn't have anyone coming or going. Cars lined the streets, but Harper didn't see anyone walking along the sidewalk as she crossed over the block. She did notice that many of the buildings held "for rent" or "For Lease" signs in the windows. Passing two bars and a questionable building receiving renovations, she gathered that most of the shops had moved out of the downtown area or were in the midst of renovations. The upstairs of the three-story buildings looked occupied, though, so people lived here but didn't shop here anymore.

In the front of Ames Antiques, she noticed the grimy glass window, grungy even. Her granddaddy had always cleaned the glass first thing Sunday mornings. Even the "Open" sign in the front window looked faded and cracked. Just because it was an antique store didn't mean the store had to look like it had been unearthed from the 1800s.

Overhead, a bell jangled her arrival. Her granddaddy had always insisted he should greet his customers and not an annoying bell. The jarring to her jaw agreed with her granddaddy.

Harper inhaled sharply as she took in the general dishevelment of the shop. Items were strewn everywhere—tables, floor, and racks. Many items looked like trash instead of antiques. Upon closer inspection, she could tell that the vase on the table was a cheap retail store imitation of Chinese pottery. Anyone with a trained eye would know this.

Albert emerged from the back storeroom with his glasses hanging from the bridge of his nose. "Can I help you?"

Harper pointed to the vase. "This isn't real." Albert glanced at the vase and frowned. Pointing to the window, Harper said, "When's the last time you cleaned the window?"

Albert stared at her, his lips parting in puzzlement. "I'm sorry."

Harper weaved through the mounds of items. "This is my grandfather's shop."

"Ah." He nodded, his glasses dangling precariously on the tip of his nose, threatening to abandon this place as well. "Must be one of the little ones that moved away. I don't remember your face."

"Harper Ames," she said, handling a Hummel figurine. It shouldn't be in the store. Granddaddy had collectors on a list that wanted to be called when he'd find an item like this— collectors who would pay.

"I do remember you." He scanned the items, looking out above his glasses. "Always trailing behind your grandfather as he taught you about the shop."

Harper set the Hummel back onto the shelf. "Did he leave you as manager?"

"Well, no," he said, pushing his glasses up his nose. "He didn't, but about three months after he retired, Sissy opened the café next door and appointed me manager."

"Next door?" How convenient for her.

Harper turned to leave. "I plan to bring my granddaddy to visit real soon. He's missed this place."

"Really?" His eyes darted around the shop. Harper imagined he was taking in the mess he'd made of things.

"Yes," she said sharply, before leaving the way she'd come.

The downtown brick three story structures shared a wall, so assuming she needed to continue forth to find the café, Harper walked along the sidewalk until she'd reached the change in brick color—dusty mauve to white. On the sparkling clear window, glass red script letters read Bittersweet. Black-checkered valances offered a nice contrast against the shiny red metal bistro tables inside. On the back wall, clearly legible from the window, a chalkboard style menu held individual white letters spelling out food choices.

Sissy had put tremendous effort into creating an inviting place. From the occupied tables and the line nearly reaching the door, it appeared as if it had become successful.

In all her efforts though, she'd sacrificed the antique shop her grandparents had entrusted her with two years ago when Granddaddy retired. Harper wondered if that's who Sissy had become.

Emmett

Emmett motioned again for the bartender as he glanced back at the corner booth he and his friend had confiscated for the night. Long before CJ owned the place, his group of college friends had been visiting this sports bar, some time freshmen year when they had cheap knock off IDs. Emmett had stopped coming six months ago when things had begun to go south at work, which is why when he'd decided to see if he could get with Ralph on some kind of job connection, he'd missed the memo about it being couples' night now. His plan for the evening would have been different if he'd known.

The dark-haired beauty in a halter-top behind the bar made eye contact finally, and he requested the round of beers. As she began uncapping the bottles, Ralph tapped him on the shoulder.

Typical, sophisticated city guy, Ralph wore a blazer minus the tie to have drinks with his friends when all of the others wore old university t-shirts and jeans. "You've been quiet tonight."

Emmett shrugged. "Hard to get a word in with the ladies."

Ralph chuckled, his perfect teeth flashing and catching the eye of the bartender who smiled.

Emmett smiled politely, but he could not muster a laugh. "I was thinking about extending my job search to the city. What do you think?"

"Depends," Ralph said, winking at the barmaid as she set the bottles on the counter. Emmett and Ralph grabbed the necks and headed back toward the table. "I hate my job. I handle papers, rarely see clients, work long hours, and drive into the city because Ellie doesn't want to move where she's afraid to get robbed, according to her."

"But it's a job," Emmett said, trying to distinguish which one was Ellie at the table from this distance. His friends seemed to have a type: Blondes with thin, narrow faces that were heavily made up tonight. Only one stood out, which was Jackson's wife, a redhead with fiery green eyes who'd played softball in college. Sophie had been around since college, but back then she'd stayed away from guys' night and enjoyed her own night with her girlfriends or teammates.

"That it is," Ralph said, "but if I were you, I would give it some time and figure out what job I actually want before I go into corporate law. Take my word for it. I would get out if I could."

"Just in time," Jackson announced as Emmett placed the bottles in front of him. He grabbed one and pushed his empty long neck to the side before placing his arm back around Sophie.

A petite blonde sitting next to David giggled. "He's the best."

Emmett had noticed that she was keeping up with David in empty bottle count, and David could drink them all under the table on a good night. He didn't know if he should be impressed or worried.

"I know," Ellie said as Ralph slid in next to her. "We need to set Emmett up on a date. Who has a single friend?"

Jackson leaned back in the booth. "I've heard Harper's in town."

"Ooh, who's Harper?" the petite blonde asked, looking around the group wide-eyed.

"Childhood sweetheart," Jackson said, sipping on his beer, his eyes on Emmett.

Jackson enjoyed this talk. Perhaps the guys had grown tired of talking about sports, fishing, and work successes and would rather gossip.

Ralph sipped from his beer and cringed. "Sissy invited me to the engagement party."

"You're engaged?" the blonde squealed, leaning forward across the small table.

"No," Emmett said, keeping it cool as Jackson watched him. "Harper's fiancé is also in town."

Jackson chuckled. "There's always Sissy."

Ellie sipped from a glass of wine. "I don't like her for you. I hope this Harper isn't anything like her cousin. I'd have to question your taste, Emmett." She followed it with a conspiratory wink between the two.

Ellie remained the beauty at the table. Even with her hours in the sun, she kept her skin fair and her figure lean. Ralph had been lucky to find someone who didn't mind his occasional arrogance.

"Doesn't matter if she's engaged, right?" The blonde looked at all their faces, confused.

"She's not married yet," Jackson said, holding his beer bottle nonchalantly as if they were discussing the weather instead of Emmett's dating forecast. "Our Emmett could still stand a chance."

Emmett laughed, remembering the tense discussion he'd witnessed outside recently between Harper and Clint. "I think all your good fortune in love has given you insane ideas about romance. People don't end up with their childhood sweethearts."

David's blonde leaned into the crook of his arm. "We have been so lucky. I can't imagine being single."

Sophie perked up from Jackson's side. "I have a girl down at the gym that might be interested. I want to see this Harper first to see what's your type. At least with Sissy throwing a party, it should be a good time."

"How about we talk about something else?" Emmett said. "I hear you're finally becoming an official doctor, Sophie?"

She nodded.

At this opening, everyone moved on to discussing Sophie's new career, and Emmett could be alone in his thoughts while nestling his beer. Lately, he couldn't catch a break. Turning circumstances around in his favor was proving challenging. The job market for lawyers was saturated, and even with connections, he continued to be advised to go in a different direction. He hadn't thought about a different direction since he was twelve, as the expectation in his family had been to practice law in the family firm. But now, he didn't know how to proceed with the job hunt. Floundering around left him feeling as meaningless as Winston, and this he could not live with.

He needed something, anything. It wouldn't be at the

bottom of this beer, but perhaps perspective sat at the bottom like the old kaleidoscope he'd played with as a looking glass on his adventures with Harper as a kid.

Harper

Walking down the hall to where her grandfather's office was nestled against the back of their bedroom, she attempted to shake off the night's aggravation. Dinner with Clint and her grandparents had proven to be a challenge. He'd decided charming them would be a way to get back into Harper's good graces. All dinner long he'd regaled them with stories of their fun times, but none of his stories included anything from the last year and a half. Currently, he was telling stories to Grams in the kitchen and helping with the dishes—something she wasn't sure he even knew how to do.

Harper needed a place to take a deep breath and get her head together.

On the wall in the hall, Harper glanced at the collage of photos. In her youth, she'd never paid much attention to them. A particular old circular frame with opaque glass caught her attention. The woman must be Grand-mère Amelia. She vaguely recalled the stories of the dark-haired beauty from France that had been sent over to marry Grand-père Florian. The string of opalescent pearls was a telling sign that she was correct. Pearls that had disappeared during the Civil War when the boys had gathered all the jewelry. The stories said that she never took them off. Harper wondered how the boys got them. Something to remember to ask Granddaddy, if he could remember that tidbit of history.

Stooped over his desk, her granddaddy was drawing lines on a map rolled out on the surface. Several items were spread out across his area as though he wanted the journal and envelopes at his fingertips.

He glanced up as she approached, a smile deepening. "Harper, you've come to join in the treasure hunting? I think we are making progress."

Harper walked around the desk so she could clearly read the markings. The map held sketches of the house and the buildings on the property. Granddaddy had made several marks near some of the buildings as well as shaded some areas gray. As far as she could tell, the gray spots were areas he'd dug and had discovered nothing. The amount of area remaining to cover felt overwhelming. Harper had to admire his dedication and perseverance.

But her realistic mind dwelled in the hopelessness of the task. He'd never find these family heirlooms as the pieces of his memory became more fragmented.

"What is your next location?" Harper asked, looking over the map.

"I believe it will be here." He pointed a stiff finger to an area near her mother's old home, Sissy's house now, where a cistern once stood. The old cistern had been moved ages ago to a backfield to hold water for cows. Since the car accident, though, the family leased the property to a sugarcane farmer. Most of the year, the stalks blocked the view of that point in the horizon where all those flashing lights had once signaled the turn of the tide for her life. After that point, everything became pre-mother's murder or after mother's murder.

She moved around to get the image from returning to the forefront of her mind, and the old battle models on the tables against the far wall caught her attention.

Her granddaddy had built a miniature model of the battle of Lafourche Crossing, complete with soldiers. He'd put all the nearby structures to show the entire area. As a child, it had been difficult to keep her hands from playing with it when she was itching to act out dramatic death scenes and escapes, but her granddaddy would only laugh. For him, it was a way to see the history and visualize the time period after having listened to all the stories of his own grandfather.

She walked over to the one in the middle. "Do you still work on these?"

Granddaddy remained silent, so she glanced back at him to see him puzzling over the models as he looked upon them.

"I remember you working on these when I was young," she rushed on, covering the silence.

"Yes," he uttered. "I built those. I've been digging though. No time for models."

Harper offered him a reassuring smile.

Grams entered the study with a glass of water and a small plastic container. "No digging on Sundays, Walter. It's a day of rest."

Granddaddy winked. "Oh, my wife still keeps me in line with

the Lord after all these years, even though I can't remember the day of the week."

He chuckled and took the medication without hesitation.

"The Lord may forgive us if we scout instead. What do you say, Grams?" Harper said, smiling at the woman. She couldn't allow Granddaddy's momentum to slow down.

"You are a bad influence, Harper Marie Ames," Grams said. "But I can pray for two just as easily as one."

Granddaddy winked at her again. "She was raised right, just like her granddaddy."

Harper laughed as Grams regarded her with doubt. "Have you been down to the antique store recently?" Harper asked, not knowing how to broach the subject of its condition with them without insulting Sissy.

Grams shook her head. "It's been too much. Sissy assures us that everything is fine."

Harper walked toward an empty chair near Granddaddy's desk. "How are profits?"

Granddaddy drew a mark on his map. "Like the Roman sewers."

Grams frowned and twiddled with a curl that had escaped her tight updo. "Sissy says most of the stores downtown are closed and business is slow right now, but with the revitalization, things should turn around soon."

Harper arched her eyebrow at her grams, and she shrugged. The woman continued, "Your grandfather refuses to sell, and Sissy is the only one who will run it."

"Sell what, darling?" Granddaddy asked.

"The store."

"Ah," he said, leaning back in his brown leather wingback chair. "I need to pull that piece tomorrow for Canto. He's interested in buying, not selling like I thought when I talked to him. Someone has something they wish to sell?"

He looked at them expectantly, his eyes muddled and wiped clear of their earlier conversation. After a few days, she'd come to expect it, although it was gut clenching painful each time.

Harper thought of the piece that sat collecting dust on the shelf. "A Hummel piece."

"Did Shelia Fairgood finally decide to get rid of her collection?" he asked, eyebrows furrowed as he looked at the papers in front of him, puzzling over what he was looking at with the spread out items. "She should fetch a good price for them."

Grams patted him on the shoulder. "How about you turn in for the night? I think you and Harper will be busy tomorrow."

"Oh yeah?" Granddaddy winked. "Are we expecting a big crowd at the store tomorrow?"

Harper smiled. All of this just compounded and became another sign that he would never discover the Ames treasure.

Harper followed Grams and Granddaddy toward the door.

"Where did you leave Clint?" she asked, suddenly imagining the man wandering around the house unattended.

Grams walked alongside Granddaddy, a hand out at the ready in case he needed assistance. "He retired early to get an early start on party planning tomorrow. I'm so happy that we get to be part of this, Harper."

Harper studied her granddaddy as he rubbed at his head and then his chin. "Don't you think it's too much for him?"

"It's perfect," Grams said. "We could all use a little joy in our lives right now."

Harper's chest throbbed. How would she ever tell the truth?

Emmett

"It's time to flip, Emmett," Mr. Richard Ames said as he stepped aside to avoid the smoke from the grill. "It's all about the timing."

Sissy's father had decided that he'd teach them how to grill the perfect burger this afternoon, but Emmett would rather be wandering around the yard with Harper and Mr. Walter helping out with the tape measure. Everyone else had lost interest in watching them after ten minutes, but Emmett yearned for the days when it had been acceptable for him to not be one of the adults.

Clint sat huddled in one of the wicker chairs, his nose in a textbook. Occasionally, the man would pop his head over the cover to comment on a topic, but everyone let him be. Sissy, on the other hand, continued to drag Emmett into the conversation, forcing him to follow the thread of the talk around him instead of stare off into the field like he'd prefer.

"Maybe we could cook for some of our friends out here, Emmett," Sissy gushed. "Maybe even out by the little house."

Emmett studied her. The way she avoided direct eye contact, the way she kept inching closer to him, the way she kept speaking as if there was a "we," all spoke of a hidden agenda. He'd been surprised this morning by the invite, figuring he wouldn't be included much in the social order while Harper visited. Not that there was open animosity between the two, but an awkwardness of words spoken you couldn't take back sat in the air between them. After listening to Sissy, Emmett was getting the picture of why he'd been invited today.

He'd underestimated Sissy's desire to compete with Harper. Since he'd known the two, there'd always been a competitive streak. From who would get first in a race or who would have the better grades to who'd be the best at any activity they'd taken on—they'd tried to outdo each other. The distance of living hundreds of miles away from each other for a decade had only increased the stakes.

Emmett let Sissy's comment slide, and the conversation turned toward other cookouts that the Ames family had hosted back when everyone was younger.

Richard twirled the spatula in his hand. "How's the job hunt going?"

Emmett pulled himself away from Sissy's story of the disastrous Independence Day picnic. Effie, Sissy's mother, told the story with Sissy's assistance in her shrill, nasally voice.

"Not very well, Sir." Emmett frowned, feeling Richard's scrutiny. "There's an overabundance of lawyers these days."

"Always too many of those." Richard chuckled. "I'd suggest you try business or finance or something more lucrative in these economic times. I could get you in with our financial company, but Franklin Hebert would have a stroke if an Hebert came to work for an Ames."

Emmett nodded. He'd always appreciated how the family did not hold the sins of his father and grandfather against him, but he could do without the subtle ribbing right now when he remained sore that the two Hebert men had put him in this current predicament. Of course Richard didn't know this, so Emmett shouldn't really hold it against him.

Sissy patted his leg. "You're a lawyer. It's who you are. You'll figure it out."

She sounded almost possessive of it, as if it were her accomplishment, too.

Maybe he should leave before Sissy complicated things between them.

"A man isn't his job," Mr. Walter said, shuffling onto the back porch with Harper aiding him. "He's made up of his choices, his character."

"You got that right, Pops," Richard said. "Emmett has always made good choices."

Harper's green eyes flashed, but she remained quiet. Her eyes spoke her opinion. He didn't always make great choices. Everyone should be entitled to make mistakes, but sometimes the mistakes led to consequences you couldn't take back.

His choice at fifteen had caused the accident, and she had not forgiven him for it from the look in her eyes.

"Harper," Mr. Walter said, "what are your thoughts on the subject?"

She looked at him and smiled, any appearance of anger gone from her eyes. "I think one should do what makes one happy every day, and then the day won't feel like drudgery."

He chuckled. "I knew someone listened to me when I spoke."

Clint put his textbook down. "Unfortunately, that doesn't pay the rent."

Sissy fiddled with her messy bun at the nape of her neck. "Harper never really cared much about the practical. Always had her head in the clouds."

"Nonsense," Harper said, crossing her arms across her chest. "You figure out how to make it work."

Sissy's fist clenched on the top of her leg, and Emmett could predict an argument coming. "Is that why you were working at the bakery? I don't recall your passion being cupcakes."

"No," Harper said, slowly measuring her words. "I supported someone else's passion, but now that's done, I'm finishing my doctorate."

"How practical," Sissy said sharply. "But what about a job? Money? Rent?"

Clint squirmed in his seat. "You're going back to school? Now?"

Harper's brow furrowed as she glared at Clint, but she didn't respond to his question. Even though he hadn't spent much time with the adult version of Harper, Emmett didn't need to know more than the childhood version of Harper to see something was wrong.

"C'mon ladies," Emmett said playfully. "I thought we were talking about me and my pitiful predicament."

"Growing up you always wanted to be an adventurer," Harper said, a hint of irritation in her tone. "Figure out a way to do that."

Emmett leaned back into the folds of the cushions, feeling the tension lighten in his shoulders. Becoming a lawyer had been family expectation, as he'd come from a long line of them. No one had ever asked him what he wanted to do with his life. He could use this opportunity to do what he was good at instead of fulfill this obligation.

He didn't know about adventurer, as he'd spent too much time behind a desk; but he could figure out what he wanted to spend everyday doing. Other possibilities could be entertained.

Once, he and Harper would have draped their legs over the porch boards and tossed ideas around about his options until one of them stuck. It had been a long time since that snapshot in time, but seeing her now made him long for the simplicity of those moments again.

Harper

Grabbing a bag loaded down with grilling equipment, Harper trekked after Uncle Richard to his SUV as he loaded up the extra chairs. He turned as she approached and offered one of his big, goofy grins.

With his big lanky arms and hands, he relieved her of the bag. "Always was the helpful one. Not afraid to get your hands dirty."

She felt a twinge of guilt at the compliment, since she'd only been trying to get five minutes alone with him all afternoon to broach the subject of the antique store.

She kicked her toe on a lone rock in the sandy parking pad. "I was never big on the afternoon gossip sessions."

He chuckled. "I imagine not. You spent too much time with the old man growing up."

Harper leaned against the SUV, hoping to get him to pay attention. "I was actually wondering about Granddaddy. Are there any plans to get him more help? I mean Grams more help?"

He shook his head, a frown tugging at the corner of his thin lips. "Mom refuses to consider a facility, and right now we have to respect her wishes. If it gets worse, of course, we will have to approach it again with her."

If it gets worse? She didn't know of any cases where dementia wasn't progressive. Clint had made sure to explain it all in clinical terms, not sparing any of the cruel details. Uncle Richard must have had these conversations already with Granddaddy's doctors. Unless their participation in his medical care had been a lie as well. She'd missed so much in her time away. There was a guilt nestled at her center that throbbed when she thought of the time she'd missed out on with her granddaddy.

She needed to focus right now, though. She could examine her feelings later.

"What about the shop then?" She said, watching her uncle closely. "I visited and saw that it has been allowed to go downhill. It can't be making a profit."

He paused in arranging the ice chest in the back to look at her with reproachful eyes. "The family has asked them to sell it. Maybe you can talk Mom into it?"

"Me?" Harper's voice croaked, wondering what family participated in that conversation. She could imagine the betrayal her granddaddy had experienced that day.

He nodded. "No one in the family wants to run the store. Everyone has their own careers, passions. Mom hopes one of us will retire and take it over, but I've just finally talked Aunt Effie into retiring from the hospital after thirty-five long years of working, and I don't want her going back to something she doesn't want to do. I want her to have time to relax and hopefully spend time with our future grandkids."

"None of the cousins want it?" Harper asked, her face burning. Granddaddy would be so angry if he knew that the business was leaving family hands. His own father had struggled to get that business off the ground. But even if they'd told him, he'd probably not remembered the conversation. Maybe that had been their plan.

"Sissy is the only one who lives in the area," he said, shutting the back hatch. "She's doing the best to help out now, but in the meantime she's found a buyer. If you can get Mom to sell, it would be the best decision for everyone."

"What if I helped out?" Harper said without thinking. Someone who was supposed to be only visiting for a week shouldn't be volunteering to run a store that would require a full time staff, but Uncle Richard wasn't typically the type to pay much attention to her life anyway.

"Don't put yourself in that situation," Uncle Richard said, a kind smile reaching his eyes. "You are getting married, and Clint wants to work in a big hospital with a trauma unit. He said so at lunch. Just think it over, and you'll see that selling while we have an interested buyer is the best for everyone."

Harper crossed her arms across her chest in a huff as Uncle Richard walked back to the house to collect his family. Best for everyone but her granddaddy. Breaking the man's already fragile heart didn't feel right.

The man who had talked entirely too much around the lunch table now strolled towards her with his hands in his pocket and his elbows held tightly against his unwrinkled, blue polo shirt. Why she hadn't given up this pretense yet, she didn't know.

She couldn't stomach the idea of disappointing her grandparents though, and she knew that the truth would be devastating as Grams appeared excited about the idea of a party to cheer up Granddaddy.

"What are you doing out here?" He asked, looking around at the neglected cars. "I looked for you after everyone went inside, and I couldn't find you."

Harper began walking briskly back toward the house. "You needed something?"

Clint reached out and tugged on her arm. "Wait, I thought you and I could talk. I feel like we haven't had a moment alone since I arrived."

This was completely by design, but it was just like Clint not to see it. There was a time he would have caught on to her strategy, but that was at the beginning of the relationship when he'd showered her with interest.

"Clint..." She sighed. She needed to end this charade. Perhaps Grams could throw a party for Granddaddy for another reason. "I don't think this is going to work. I'm just going to tell my grandmother the truth, and we can end this... whatever this is."

He gripped her hand tightly in his. "Please, Harper, I can't lose you. You're my best friend. Your family loves me. Just give me a chance to make up for my mistake."

"It's a big mistake, don't you think?"

"I know." He hung his head, remorse weighing heavily. "Please don't end everything yet. If you tell your family, they will hate me. We will never have a chance after they know what I did, and you know it. I can do better."

Harper looked into his sad, pleading face. He really believed that they could work it out. He believed that she had it in her to forgive him.

But the betrayal still twisted inside of her. He'd cheated on her with a man. All the right words and heartfelt actions couldn't erase what she'd seen for herself. And forgiveness did not come easy for her. She had this anger festering inside of her from her mother's death that snuffed out all chances of forgiveness for anyone else. She knew that this was unhealthy and probably didn't bode well for relationships, but she clung to the familiarity of the hard shell she'd built around herself. But if she took Clint out of the equation, and she considered Granddaddy and Grams's happiness—they wanted a party. And she couldn't think of a way to break her grandparents' heart and tell them that there would be no party—at least not an engagement party.

"Okay," Harper said, "I will hold off telling my family for the time being, but don't talk about wedding dates or anything like that with them. We are not getting married this summer."

His eyes lit up with triumph. "It would be great timing though with me accepting a new position in the fall."

The urge to revoke the decision, to wipe it away, swelled up inside of her instantly, but she knew there was enough going on at the moment to allow it to fester a little while longer. She could wait a few weeks to add a broken engagement to the string of items that were ruined in her life right now.

Harper walked toward the house, breaking free of the grasp he had of her hand. "I'm not moving away. I'm going to finish my doctorate before I make any more plans for the future."

Clint stepped in front of her. "What if my position is in North Carolina though?"

Harper's heart skipped. "Is it?" This could force her to make an immediate decision. In an instant, she knew she wasn't ready to do it.

Clint smiled. "It's a possibility. Just think, a fellowship that you helped me achieve. You can do whatever you want then. Stay home and have a baby, whatever."

Harper gulped against the urge to slap him, stretching her fingers out as they clenched up. Her eight-year-old inner child was angry that she didn't at least stomp on his toes when she walked away from him, leaving him staring at her, terrified to follow from just her facial expression.

Emmett

Taking the stairs two at a time, he was nearly at the top before he heard the voices speaking in hushed, somber tones. At the door to his room, he paused, curious as to who would visit Winston, especially in his current condition. Typically, the man didn't entertain socially when he was sober, and certainly not during a binge.

With his hand on his own door, he considered taking the few steps down the hall to quench his curiosity, but he didn't feel like dealing with Winston, who would only dampen his mood.

But then a short brunette emerged out of the room, and he was standing face-to-face with his mother. In jeans and a white t-shirt, she looked youthful still, even though he could see crinkles forming at the corners of her eyes.

"What are you doing here?" he asked. The oddness of seeing her— in his father's bedroom no less — had caught him off guard.

She smiled, the creases deepening. "It's good to see you. I thought I might miss you when Winston said you were next door."

Her hands fidgeted against her sides as if she were nervous.

She hadn't called to make plans to see him, and it didn't make sense to him to see her in this house.

He peered around her toward Winston's room as if he could see through walls and ajar doors. "Is something wrong?"

She stepped closer to him but then hesitated to come closer. "Nothing's wrong with your brothers. Your dad called to talk. I think he just needed some... well, anyway, he's struggling right now."

Emmett felt his face heat and darken. He couldn't imagine why this woman would make excuses for that man. "He's been struggling my entire life."

"You should really go easy on him," she spoke softly. "He's been through quite a bit."

Emmett's spine straightened. Winston did not need another person enabling him, and certainly not the woman he'd gotten pregnant in high school and promptly abandoned. "Is that all?"

She frowned, tiny creases forming at the corners of her lips. She was only seventeen years older than him. As a teenager when he'd finally gone somewhere with her, they'd been mistaken for siblings. It had been infuriating after years of her neglecting him. When the creases had begun, he'd felt vindicated. At least she would appear motherly, if not having behaved motherly. He should feel horrible about this pettiness existing inside of him, and sometimes he did feel guilty. At other times, he just swallowed the guilt.

She reached out and brushed his arm. "The boys have a baseball game Thursday. I'm sure they'd love for you to come."

"I think I'm busy that night," he said, bristling at her touch. "I'll check my schedule and let you know."

"Okay," she said, casting her eyes down. "It was good seeing you, Son."

She brushed past him, squeezing his arm as she went. He didn't flinch against her touch. After all the years without her, it felt strange any time she attempted to be motherly, especially now when he was thirty years old.

"Nice to know it's not just me you treat like shit." Winston stood in the doorway, his unshaven face, unbrushed hair, and wrinkled clothing appearing quite rough.

"What can I say?" Emmett said, throwing open his door, irritated. "I blame it on the parenting."

Winston shook his head. "You don't know anything, Kid. Keep living in that bubble of yours."

He disappeared back into the cloud of stench that by this point the walls had absorbed and would need to be repainted or the room gutted to purge the room of the nasty funk wafting into the hall.

Emmett should let it go. Winston was trying to get a rise out of him, that's all. Something he was good at these days, especially now that they shared quarters.

But, dammit, what did he mean by it?

He had to know.

Following Winston inside his bedroom, he resisted pulling his shirt up over his face to breathe through instead of the foul odor of sweat, bodily fluids, and stale cigarettes.

"What are you talking about?"

Winston chuckled. "Trust me, you don't want to know. You may realize how much like your old man you really are, and it may knock you off that pedestal you've placed yourself on."

Emmett frowned. He didn't like to be toyed with, and Winston had a way of doing just that. "I'm nothing like you."

"Oh yeah?" Winston said, throwing himself atop the crumpled bed. "From what I just saw of how you treated your mother, you acted just like the old man and me. That woman doesn't deserve that."

"And what does she deserve?" Emmett asked, feeling anger rise at his reproach. "She left me with Gramps when I was a year old while both my parents went off to college and pretended they didn't have a kid. They didn't even visit on weekends. And then they graduate and move on and keep right on pretending. How am I supposed to treat someone like that since you seem to be so keen on telling people the correct way?"

"The fact that you still believe that shows how classy a woman your mother is," Winston said smugly.

Emmett just stared at him, not trusting his anger to speak any more.

Winston shrugged his shoulders. "Just consider what happens every time I screw up. What does your gramps do? Do you think that it started with the accident?"

Emmett gritted his teeth. "What did he do?"

"Ask the old man," Winston said, leaning back against the pillows. "I want to see if he has the guts to tell you."

Emmett stared at him a moment longer, knowing it was no use. He was as stubborn a man as he was a drunk.

"Take care of your own life, Winston," Emmett said. "Do something—anything really—and stop acting like a teenager blaming his father for everything that's gone wrong."

"Good advice, Son," Winston said. "I'd take it if I were you."

Emmett walked out, unable to dismiss what Winston had implied. He had this terrible feeling that he'd been missing something important, and he didn't think he'd like what it was.

Harper

The smell of baking chocolate had drifted through the house and had found her in the alcove where she'd tucked herself away reading about the battle of Lafourche Crossing in a book her granddaddy had placed in her hands last night with instructions to gather the story. Since he'd felt rather tired much of the morning and had gone to lie down after lunch, she'd figured she'd give the local author a shot. It wasn't like she'd discover a thesis by mulling around and trying to figure out a new life for herself.

The overpowering aroma, though, interrupted her quest for the story her granddaddy had spoken, and she wandered into the kitchen to see what her grams had concocted.

A strange gentleman hovered over the island unlidding containers and sticking spoons into shiny metal dishes. His white apron and thick hat emanated a professional vibe.

Sissy turned from her hovering, take-charge stance. "Well, there you are. I thought I would have to form a search party."

Harper saw a plate of her grams's brownies pushed aside on the counter, wondering if they were for a special occasion.

"What's going on?" Grams sat in the corner rocking rhythmically in her rocking chair, watching the activity of the room.

"The taste testing, silly," Sissy said, waving her hand at the gentleman as if she were on a game show revealing a grand prize. "I told you it would be at 3:00 today."

Harper studied Sissy. She had a fake smile plastered across her rouge lips, but it didn't reach her eyes. "I think I would have remembered that appointment."

"There you are," Clint said, coming up behind her. Instinctively, Harper stepped to the side as he brushed up against her. "It slipped my memory when Sissy told me yesterday, but what else do we have to do right now that's more important?"

Harper clenched her jaw, but smiled for the stranger's benefit, not wanting to make the situation awkward.

Sissy laughed. "Fantastic. Guys, this is my friend Javier Decampo. He's a wonderful caterer who specializes in tailored menus. He's brought a few tasting samples for us so that we can put the engagement party menu together."

"Oh," Clint said, hovering over the island, eyeing each dish. "I skipped lunch so that I could enjoy all of this."

Harper walked over to the old chair next to her grams and sank into it. The old woman patted Harper's hand with a frail hand of blue spider web veins.

"I came for the brownies," Harper whispered.

Grams laughed.

Sissy glanced in their direction. "Did you say something?" Her right manicured hand automatically went to her hip.

Seeing the agitation playing at the corner of Sissy's lips, Harper smiled. "I can't wait for dessert."

"I suggest this warm arugula salad as a first course," Javier spoke, a soft accent seeping through his carefully pronounced words as if he'd practiced tireless hours to erase a language besides English from his vocabulary.

Sissy and Clint took the small paper plates he handed to them. Harper waited until he moved toward her and her grams before she finally looked into his dark black eyes peering out from a chic of black curled hair on his forehead. He couldn't be long out of culinary school, if he wasn't still a student.

She thanked him for the crisp arugula salad adorned with pecans and bits of strawberries. At first bite, the dressing was tart, but as it moved around her palate a hint of sweetness rolled around.

Not bad, but her idea of a party menu for a backyard party would have consisted of grilled meat, potato salad, deviled eggs, her Aunt Vivian's strawberry fluff dessert, and the homemade ice cream her granddaddy would make in his machine. Fancy arugula salad had never been served at an Ames party, and she could imagine the upturned noses and puzzled faces of the family when they stood in the buffet line.

"This is great," Clint said between bites. "An excellent choice for a starter."

Harper noticed that Grams set hers down on the bistro table between them, having only taken a bite. Likely the same reaction from a majority of the aunts and uncles.

Javier began distributing larger size plates with an array of colors in small piles.

As he approached Harper and Grams, his hands shook, revealing his nerves and inexperience. "For the entrée, I've prepared several options."

Harper thanked him for the offering while her grams only smiled.

"This fettuccini is fabulous," Sissy said, a fork raised to her lips. "I think that should be the choice since everyone will love that dish."

"I'll vote for the gumbo," Harper whispered.

Grams smiled as she poked at the fettuccini with her fork. Harper couldn't blame her. It tasted nothing like Great Aunt Izzy's, who made the best in the family—the best Harper had ever tasted. Great Aunt Izzy wouldn't divulge her much sought after recipe, treasuring the fact that everyone wanted her to bring it to family gatherings, but she was ninety-two now, so hopefully she'd written it down.

"Which one do you like?" Harper asked, leaning in to speak quietly to her grams.

Grams shook her head. "It's not about me, Sweetheart. It's your day."

Harper stared at the food and sighed. This was all wrong. There would be no day. This was all a horrible farce because she couldn't bear to admit the truth. She needed to come clean to her grams.

Clint stood before her, catching her off guard. "Taste the chicken. I think our friends from the city will just fall in love with that dish."

Harper swallowed against the lump in her throat. "Will they drive in for this party?"

"Of course," Clint said, waving his fork around. "I've already invited them all. They can't wait to celebrate."

"Wonderful," Harper muttered under her breath. That could make calling it off more difficult.

"I know," Clint said, his eyes flickering over Grams. "Tara didn't return my calls though. You may want to give her a call."

Tara. When she'd returned here reeling from the Clint and Felipe spectacle, she and Tara had plans to meet at the wedding dress shop. Tara's take-charge, organized mind believed the dress would spur other decisions that needed to be made for a wedding to take place. In a moment of weakness, Harper had agreed. But in her mad rush to pack her things that morning, she'd left Tara only a cryptic message with not much explanation. Saying those words aloud just couldn't be done in that moment, and Harper had avoided her phone—all messages and all calls. Tara would have expected more of an explanation by now.

Sissy clicked her lips together. With a hand on hip, she peered at Harper as though she chastised her for getting off topic. "Javier has breads with various flavored butter as well. This garlic cinnamon one is divine."

"I need to try that," Clint said, turning away from Harper. "I bet it will pair nicely with this chicken."

Grams rocked back in her chair. "Clint seems excited about the party."

He did appear quite enamored with the food and the idea of a party, which wasn't the typical Clint of the latter relationship years. She couldn't confidently pinpoint what was going on with him. Guilt over a mistake? Regret over ruining a relationship? Something else?

She wanted to give him credit for effort, but she clenched every time she remembered what he'd done—which was nearly every minute of her day. She didn't want to be that person who only saw the negative though. Five years ago he'd seen her through the rough patch of losing her father. The cancer had been quick and invasive. By the time her busy father had discovered it, the cells had moved from prostate to lungs to lymph nodes. She'd had three weeks to face the reality, and Clint had put everything on hold for her then.

She and Clint had survived having only enough money to scrape together for a package of Ramon noodles as they'd waited for exam results and medical internship appointments. Even now, they joked about if rent left enough change to buy a bottle of wine. They'd spent nights talking about when life would be different.

He'd been her go-to person for six years, and he'd changed it all in thirty seconds.

"You hear that, Harper?" Sissy asked, now standing in front of her. "Clint and I decided that us four are going to go on a double date."

Harper raised an eyebrow. "Really?" That sounded like an awful idea.

"It's all decided." Sissy smiled, raising her chin proudly. "So is the food. Clint has very good taste."

Harper exhaled slowly through her teeth as that relaxation class had taught—the only technique she could ever recall from the class she and Clint had taken for a few laughs.

Of course, Clint had made all the decisions. He'd been forcing decisions more and more. And, of course, trying to keep the peace, she had let him for almost everything from the much too expensive apartment (so they could have the right sort of neighbors) to her sitting out a semester to save money and write her thesis (which had grown into years as she'd worked to pay the rent). If she had questioned his choices, he'd give her some spiel about how he had their future in mind.

Grams patted her hand. "How about I make some of my brownies for the occasion? Your granddaddy will love them."

Harper looked into Grams's eyes and saw her need to have something tangible for Granddaddy where the family could all surround him and offer a memory that perhaps he could cling to when all the other remnants of the past were falling away. It drove every decision Grams allowed to happen with this party; otherwise, there'd be a backyard cookout like the Ames tradition.

"You don't need to cook, I told you," Sissy said, her hand returning to her hip as her forehead wrinkled.

Harper smiled. "That would be perfect, Grams."

Sissy glowered.

Good. Harper needed to figure out a way to ruin these party plans. It had all grown out of hand. But she needed to do it without disappointing her grandparents.

Emmett

Clutching the roses tighter as he stumbled over the uneven growing sugarcane rows, he reconsidered his decision to do this. Bringing flowers to Beth Ames's cross marking the accident had been his grammy's weekly ritual. Since Harper's mother's body had been on their property, his grandmother would clip roses from her bushes and walk to this back spot and place them at this crude white marker. After his grammy's death, he'd thought about it going undone, letting the ritual die, but it felt as much a part of his grandmother as Beth Ames. He could ask the Ames family to continue, but it was possible the Ames family didn't know that the marker existed. For Emmett, the cross marked the change of life, a twist of fate which would lead him and others down a different path than they'd planned.

But had the defining moment been as he'd always believed?

If Winston was telling the truth, something else had occurred. Something that caused an uneasy dread to tumble around in his gut. He needed to know, but he was fearful of what the truth would do to his perceptions of the people surrounding him.

So deep in his own thoughts was he, he didn't realize that Harper stood completely still looking out over the headstone until he came upon her.

She turned toward him, her eyes watery under the glaring overhead sun.

She searched his face, her bottom lip trembling. "Why do you have this here?"

He moved toward the marker, not wanting to look at her too closely. "My grandmother did it." He placed the roses down, pulling the wilted dried up ones away. "She brought roses every week from her garden."

"And what? You've just continued?" Defensiveness had slipped into her voice. Her breathing filling the quiet field.

"It felt like the right thing to do."

He looked at her, not avoiding her hard stare. For a moment they looked into each other's eyes, and it all sat between them in the spring breeze, blanketing them like the Louisiana humidity.

Her eyes softened. "Your grandmother was a good woman."

He nodded. "The best."

She smiled. "I loved her blackberry turnovers. They'd stain your teeth purple."

"Our fingers were stained purple for weeks when we'd pick blackberries for her."

Harper looked down at her fingers, seeing something he didn't. "Why do people get old?"

Emmett shrugged. "My superpower to freeze time hasn't come in yet."

"I'd rather be able to go back and change the past," Harper said, her green eyes looking up at him through thick eyelashes.

Fifteen years were swept away, and he was standing at that back door wanting to say so much, but it was all stuck in his throat.

"I wish…" He began, not knowing where to go with that statement. He wished so many things.

Harper's green eyes clouded. "Don't. I'm sure we would both change things from back then, but it's too late. We need to move on now."

He could see her defenses returning. He wanted to bring them down again, to have her look at him and not see that day.

"I hear we are going on a double date," Emmett said, attempting to lighten the mood, return that light to her eyes.

A frown tugged at the corner of Harper's lips. "Sissy and Clint appear to get along very well. I don't remember her being… well, quite so Sissy, I suppose."

He laughed, thinking how often he'd mediated between the two when they were young. It amazed him how the distance had led the two women to forget that even back then they were different. "She's unique, but she's not so bad. Once, you two were really close."

Harper's eyes narrowed for a moment, but a moment later she returned to neutral. He wondered what that was about. He could ask, but he didn't dare upset this peace they seemed to be working towards.

He'd missed her.

He felt it now that he stood so close to her and couldn't ask her for her thoughts. Wanting to confide in her about his father, but not being able to do so made him ache for that easiness that they'd enjoyed. Rationally, he knew that they'd been too young, but he knew the connection had been there. He'd been so certain back then that he'd spend his life with her.

"Sissy wants to sell my grandfather's shop."

She watched him closely as she spoke, weighing his reaction, he could tell.

"She spoke of it once," Emmett said, nodding. "But, I thought someone had ruled it out. It's your inheritance after all."

Harper took a step back. "It's what?"

Emmett realized he'd misspoken instantly. Sissy's words from one of her tirades came back to him in a rush, and the shock on Harper's face brought the entire conversation to the forefront of his memory. "I'm sorry. I wasn't supposed to say that. I really wasn't supposed to say that."

Sissy would be furious. There would be high-pitched yelling. For a thin, petite thing she could be quite vicious when in a tear. And even though they weren't dating, she served as his connection to the Ames family, a family he needed most days to feel normal, especially with the absence of his grammy.

Harper laughed. "You sounded like we were eight years old."

Emmett laughed with her. It felt so good to hear the sound, and it echoed into the open expanse of the field.

She sobered up and looked at him, a faint smile still present. "Is there a reason you aren't supposed to tell me that?"

Emmett felt warm, but he knew it was from the hot water he'd just dunked himself head first into. "Sissy said something about your grandmother not wanting you to feel obligated to come back to this place. Mr. Walter did the giving though."

Harper nodded, bleary-eyed. "If a girl is trying to figure out what to do with her life, this certainly opens up the possibilities."

A jolt went through Emmett. Harper coming home? His mind ran over his own possibilities if this happened.

"Clint would practice medicine here?" Emmett asked. Possibilities had limits when others were involved.

Harper kicked at the grass with the tip of her shoe. "Let's leave that discussion for another time. What about you? Any job prospects yet?"

Emmett shook his head. "I think I'm the male version of you, trying to figure out what to do with my life."

As she studied her mother's marker, he stared at her unhindered. Her mother had been gone for half her life and the pain of it still contorted her face. The woman had been a great mother, always willing to create some kind of adventure for her curious daughter. Emmett had missed having a mother around a little less with Beth Ames including him in her mothering.

What if he'd missed out on his own mother for some other reason than she didn't want him?

It constricted his gut, a tight sickness curling a fist around his insides.

He remembered the animalistic pain uncurling from Harper the night she'd come to confront his family. Had the arm's distance he'd kept his mother at and the rare visit caused a similar pain to his own mother? Winston had said he didn't know the whole truth, but Emmett's actions had been based on what he'd believed was his mother's neglect. What didn't he know?

Had he caused pain to his own mother as his father and grandfather had to Harper?

The tight ropes crushing his gut tightened more.

"What if I'm as bad as my family?" He uttered aloud, the idea welling up inside him until it spilled over.

Harper swiftly turned to look up at him. He saw his pain reflecting in her eyes, and he wanted to turn away. He couldn't share his thoughts with her. He wanted to get her to forgive him not believe he was a horrible person.

She flew at him, closing in the few feet. She wrapped her arms around his chest in a hug.

He felt the numbness give way and grow into the warmness of her body. As the blood settled from his ears, he could hear her muttering. "You are a good person. I'm sorry I told you otherwise. You are a good person. I'm sorry I told you otherwise."

Harper

The cacophony of voices in the restaurant drowned out any chance of an intimate conversation, even though the table's candle flame flickering against the warm brick and burnt orange fresco style wall implied such ambience. Focusing on the people at Harper's table created a challenge when other couples hosted such animated conversations that called her away from the situation she didn't wish to be part of anyway.

Clint peered over the top of his menu. "Is the duck good? I'm surprised to see it on a menu at a restaurant of this scale."

Sissy nodded her head. "The chef here is fabulous. A culinary genius."

Emmett placed his menu down in front of him. "He can shoot a pretty good game of pool once he has a few shots of whiskey in him, too. I owe him a rematch one of these days."

Harper smiled, trying to follow the conversation, but a woman at the next table had just laughed loudly at a joke— the end of an office story she'd heard most of to escape the last five minutes of awkward silence at their own table. Before Clint's running menu commentary, she'd been intently listening to the joke to see who had taped the keys on the keyboard down and how they'd gotten caught.

Sissy placed her elbows on the table and leaned forward. "So Clint tells me that perhaps you will be moving to North Carolina?"

Harper frowned and glanced over at Clint who didn't return her look, choosing to closely study the menu instead. "Clint's considering it, but I'm not."

"Curious," Sissy said, smiling as she raised her wine glass to her lips. "How does that work? The long distance thing?"

"I don't know." Harper shrugged. "We haven't tried it. I've heard that you want to sell the shop, but I'm sure that couldn't be true either."

Sissy's wrinkle in the middle of her forehead deepened. "Granddaddy won't be around forever. Eventually, we will need to do something with it."

"Come on, ladies," Emmett interjected. "Let's have a nice evening with no bickering."

Clint emerged from his menu, still avoiding Harper's cool gaze. "So how did you two lovebirds meet?"

"Oh, you don't remember the story?" Harper said, twirling the edge of her white napkin with her finger. "The three of us all grew up together. Emmett was my childhood sweetheart."

She'd meant it as a joke, but her face flushed as Emmett bit down on his lip to prevent a smile. Perhaps it was the wine or maybe Emmett's proximity to her after his nearness yesterday. Yesterday, she didn't know what had come over her—the vulnerability in his eyes, the hopelessness she'd felt standing where her mother had taken her last breath, alone. Whatever it was, it wouldn't, couldn't happen again. Sissy seemed to have claws out and dug firmly into him as he tried to smooth everything over for Sissy between the two of them. Clint was enough to handle in the relationship department. She didn't need to get involved in any more drama right now.

Clint looked to Emmett. "Well, that makes things a little awkward. I didn't realize you were my competition." Clint smiled as if he'd never take him as a serious threat. "And I liked you."

Sissy frowned, crossing her arms across her chest, her bangles jangling. "They were kids, and it's not as if that's even mature love. Don't be so dramatic, Harper. Besides, Emmett's family lives next door, so *we* all grew up *together*."

"Oh, I love that formal brick structure," Clint said, nodding approvingly. "It gives off the air of being intimidating and stoic, unlike these old romantic plantation homes."

Emmett tapped his fork on his menu. "My grandfather would be thrilled with that impression as that's what he was going for when he had the architect design it. It's a little too cold for me."

"Nonsense," Clint said, his eyes wide. "It lets people know you are somebody. My first home is going to look like that after all this work I've put into my career."

Status. People's first impression. Top priorities for Clint. He didn't mind being without now but only because he knew the future would be different. But even with the little they had now, she'd worked so hard to keep a certain status up while he worked at his internship and heaped up mounds of student loans. With the recent distance, she realized that her desires and tastes never mattered. Clint determined the definition of what success looked like in their life.

She studied him, wondering how she'd never noticed this before.

Approaching the table, a wispy but attractive waiter offered a smoldering gaze as his deep black curly hair and olive complexion appeared darker under the lighting. His deep eyes surveyed the table quickly and fell onto Clint. Clint was one of those men who oozed charm and had once left Harper reeling when he'd lay it on thick. After years of watching him in action, though, she wanted to pound him with the menu every time he opened his mouth.

"Are we ready to order?" The waiter's voice held a slight accent that caused his syllables to be thick and sexy.

"Garçon," Clint said, turning his charming voice onto the waiter. "What would you recommend?"

"If you have adventurous taste, the duck might be a fine option. It is superb." The waiter smiled when he spoke, a dimple forming on his left cheek.

"I love adventure," Clint said, winking at him. "I'll take the duck."

The waiter tilted his head in agreement. "Fine choice."

The others at the table ordered their meals while Harper studied Clint and the waiter. Clint stared at him with warm, sultry eyes, and the waiter touched his hair, his hip, his chin, all before glancing back at Clint under the cover of thick, gorgeous eyelashes.

As he walked away, Clint's eyes trailed after him.

Harper stood abruptly. "Clint, I need to speak to you in the back."

"Right now?" Clint looked at her, alarmed.

"Now." She placed her napkin down on the table and walked off toward the back of the restaurant. As she scanned the area, all she could see were bathroom signs, no party room as she'd hoped. With Clint following on her heels, she made the hasty choice to enter the men's restroom, counting on Sissy not being likely to follow them inside due to her concerns over modesty.

"Harper, what are you doing?" Clint asked shocked.

She turned on him, looking over the faux alarm. "You're gay."

A balding gentleman at a urinal quickly zipped up and made a beeline for the door, not meeting their eyes.

Clint's face darkened. "I'm not gay."

Harper crossed her arms in front of her chest, huffing in frustration. Semantics. "You are attracted to men."

Clint's lips clasped tightly together.

Harper tilted her head and narrowed her eyes, a common stance she took during their arguments. "You were attracted to that waiter."

"Okay," he said. "I'm attracted to men *and* women. Are you happy now?"

He winced. His brow furrowed and his brown eyes darkened. She could see that it pained him to admit this.

"Then why are you trying to work things out with me?" She felt something inside of her shrink. She'd examine it later. Right now she needed to focus on making it through this conversation.

He grabbed her by the shoulders, his eyes pleading with her. "I love you, and I can't imagine you not being there in this future I planned for myself."

"And what about me?" Harper's insides quivered. "What about *my* future? Do I spend my future worrying if my husband is going to leave me for another man?"

He released her, a wounded look crinkling the corners of his eyes and quivering at the corners of his lips. "Please give me a chance to prove myself. I won't look at another man again if it makes you happy."

Giving that ultimatum sounded ridiculous to her. She didn't want to live with that over her head, nor did she want to deal with the worry of trusting him.

She straightened her shoulders. "I have to tell Grams that the wedding is off."

"I've already invited everyone to this party," he said, clasping her hands in his. "Please don't embarrass me like this, embarrass us like this. I know that somewhere deep inside you that you still love me. We can't call this off right now. Later, maybe, but not when everyone will want to know why."

He pleaded with his eyes and his hands and every line in his face and it clicked into place for Harper.

Even in this day and age when it was certainly acceptable to be gay, Clint himself was not ready to be gay or at least let anyone know he was gay. He'd acknowledged the reasoning behind the denial even though he perhaps didn't understand himself yet. He'd imagined a future for himself, and Harper would bet that in this future was a wife, two children, and a dog. Clint wore the same name brand slacks since high school. He had his hair cut by the same barber as when he was a child. He only used mint toothpaste. Everything was carefully selected down to the same pair of black socks he wore everyday and he never deviated, including this plan he had for his life. He was not a risk-taker. Clint was lying to himself more than he was lying to her. She could almost feel sorry for him.

Emmett

Even though Emmett continued to peek in various rooms, he knew the house was empty. Hollowness bounced around the walls from his footsteps as he walked up and down the floorboards. An empty house was an oddity. Winston and his grandfather rarely ventured forth these days. Since his grammy's death, his grandfather hadn't ventured out much. He'd avoided spending his hours in the garden and lawns where the woman had spent much of her time toiling about or sitting and reading.

Now, he typically only ventured outside to cause trouble for Mr. Walter. With that thought, Emmett hurried toward the back patio area, hoping the hunting riffle remained in the gun safe where he'd locked it away that last afternoon. He'd hidden the key within his own things, but living within the house made it difficult for anything to remain concealed.

On the back patio, his grandfather sat in an overstuffed cushion patio chair with his feet propped up. Although the usual daily newspaper was clutched in his hands, he peered out over the lawn staring off into the far distance.

Emmett released the painful breath he'd been holding. Mr.

Walter was safe this morning. Family feuds were exhausting.

His grandfather patted the seat next to him with the newspaper. "It's a beautiful day. You should join the Hebert men outside."

Emmett searched the area for Winston and noticed him hiding within the rose bushes. Watching for a moment, he saw that a pile of weeds had built up where the sweating man had tossed them as he worked.

Emmett felt like he'd walked into someone else's family.

Taking a seat in a cushioned chair, Emmett's backside felt the unforgiving hardness of the stiff cushion. Running his hand over the cushion, he realized that the furniture was new. His grandmother had hung onto the old furniture for twenty years, unwilling to give up her wicker set. When had the old man decided to shop for furniture? It was more likely that he knew someone who sold furniture, called him up, and placed an order for delivery. "I wanted to talk to you about something."

"So did I." The Judge nodded his head, a look of pride shinning in his eyes. "I spoke to Brooksy, and he said you could start in a week. All a misunderstanding, just like I told you."

Emmett leaned back into his seat, his thoughts processing that bit of news.

The Judge frowned. "You need a little more fight in you, my boy. Give him a run when he gives you a hard time instead of walk away. Show him you're an Hebert."

A tide of anger rose through Emmett. "I don't want it."

"What do you mean, Boy?" The Judge said, a frown tugging at all the deep crevices of the corners of his lips. "You need a job, don't you?"

"I'm not working for someone that had to be bribed into giving me a job." The back of his neck heated. Emmett could imagine what kind of deal had been worked out between the two, and he wanted nothing to do with it. "I don't even like the man after our encounter. Why would I want to deal with him every day?"

"Being a good lawyer doesn't make you likable," the Judge said, the tension in in his voice rising. "If you're worried about being liked, you'll never survive as a lawyer."

"I'm not worried about being liked," Emmett said. "I'm worried about liking myself. Which brings me to what I wanted to talk about." Emmett inhaled deep breaths to erase the throbbing in his head. "Why did my mother give me up? Did you have something to do with it?"

His grandfather glanced toward the rose bushes. "Why would you ask something like that? It's been thirty years. Let it be."

"Winston told me to ask."

The Judge huffed. "You're making that up. Your mother put you up to this, didn't she? That woman likes to cause trouble."

Emmett's pulse throbbed in his ear. His defenses were adding to Emmett's dread about the answer. "She doesn't know anything about this. Winston said you are always fixing his problems, and you fixed it back then. What did you fix?"

His grandfather stuck his bottom lip out, refusing to look in Emmett's direction. "I took care of my son. That's what a father does. You don't understand because you don't have children yet, but one day you will. Then you will thank me."

"What did you fix?" Emmett felt everything straining inside of him to scream, to lose his temper, but he held it together.

"She wanted to leave for college. Go away to Alabama and take you with her. She didn't care if Winston never got to see his son or your grandmother got to see her grandson. Winston had moved on by then to someone that fit in our social circle, and I couldn't let her take you."

The throbbing in his ear pulsed louder.

"What did you do?"

"I took care of my son," the Judge said, looking at him with chilling eyes. "I couldn't let Winston lose out."

The Judge turned and continued his contemplation of the property. Emmett knew that he would not reveal the details, but someone else may. It was apparent that he'd been lied to, though, and he didn't like what it meant.

Emmett stood. "Your son went off to college and forgot to come home on weekends while he partied. I was eight-years old before we lived in the same house. I missed out."

"He needed to create a life for you two." The Judge hit his hand against the arm of the chair, a red streak rising up the side of his neck as his temper flared.

"You've been making excuses for him his entire life," Emmett said. "You are Winston's problem."

Emmett walked away, back inside to the emptiness of the house where he could figure out his next move. He'd promised his grammy to take care of this man. He'd never broken a promise to her, but he felt himself teetering on the edge of failing.

Harper

The sheer volume of boxes stored in this attic was overwhelming. In fact, Harper wasn't sure how the floorboard hadn't buckled under the weight of the heavy containers and odds and ends. To her right, Uncle Richard's name was printed across a stack of boxes, followed by a stack of containers with Uncle Phillip's labels. Moving around the clutter, she located the first box labeled "Beth" as well as her old childhood rocking horse and an upright mirror that had stood in her room until she'd moved out.

Harper sank to her knees in front of a few lone boxes. When she'd come up here—escaping more party planning nonsense—she didn't have a particular item in mind she needed. Her only thought had been to assess what had been salvaged from her mother's house. With the mounds of boxes in front of her, she wondered what had not been saved.

Yanking open a cardboard box labeled "Collections," Harper peered inside to see a bag of old seashells her mother had collected from a beach trip the three of them had gone on when Harper had been five. They'd walked along the sand with Harper running ahead every time she peered a shell peeking out from the waves of sand. At least that's how her mother had told the story whenever Harper had plucked one from the crystal bowl they'd filled on the snack bar. Inside was also an old penny collection that her mother had started when she was a child. Harper had only really been fascinated by the Indian Head penny. They'd all looked the same to her, even though her mother had explained the little letters representing where they were minted.

Within a wooden box carved with a delicate moon pattern on top were the contents of her mother's antique jewelry collection. Each piece was individually wrapped in black felt, and the small collection only contained seven pieces.

Beth Ames did not have expensive taste when it came to clothing or pretty much anything else. She bought her clothes at the thrift store—she said they were going to get ruined with her work anyway. She preferred to repurpose than to buy anything new for the house, and since she could preserve antique furniture and homes, her repurposing always came out better than what you could buy in an assembly-line store.

But what she did have an eye for was antique jewelry—the kind that you saved your money over long periods of time for and had to purchase at estate auctions.

Growing up, she'd let Harper try these delicate items on and gaze at herself in the mirror as the diamonds or rubies dazzled in the light.

Harper knew every latch, every prong, and every cut of the jewels.

Great Grandmother's ring, a delicate emerald broach, a diamond bracelet, a ruby and diamond bracelet, and three very different pairs of earrings. One pair her mother always wore with her only good black dress, and another, smaller diamond set that she'd allowed Harper to wear to a Christmas dance once.

Counting the individual packets, Harper could see only six. She was recounting when a shuffling near the door drew her attention.

Sissy crinkled her nose as she looked around. "We were wondering where you disappeared to. We need your input on the music list."

Setting the six items back into the box, Harper looked around at the mounds of boxes stacked precariously, taking up the entire left corner of the attic. When her father had swept her away from here after the funeral, he'd allowed her to take two suitcases. She'd figured that everything would wait for her right where she'd left it. Counting on many visits back here, she'd planned to still count these items as hers. Truthfully, the entire concept of leaving and never coming back had not felt real when she was packing in the hour her father had granted her before their flight. When she'd unpacked and realized she'd only brought clothes and nonsense items with her, she'd sat on the strange bed in her father's cold apartment and cried.

Why she'd believed nothing would change while she was gone, she didn't know. Nothing stayed the same. Even the house, which her mom had carved out as their home hadn't always been the house of her memories. Beth Ames liked change. On a whim, she could repaint an entire wall and toss out every item in the room and redecorate. What Harper imagined when she thought of her mother and home was the one she'd been standing in when she'd looked around for the last time before wheeling her suitcase out behind her father.

"Harper?" Sissy tapped her foot on the splintered floorboards.

Closing the wooden box, Harper placed it in her lap. "Who packed up everything?"

Sissy stared at her. A slight frustration seeping into the long calculated look. "Granddaddy and my dad packed everything. I'm sure most of it's here. The furniture wasn't really worth anything as it was all…" she looked down at Harper and seemed to reconsider her thought. "Repurposed."

Harper nodded. "It's strange seeing it all in boxes."

"Well, we had to pack things away at some point," Sissy said, straightening out a nonexistent wrinkle in her shirt.

Harper raised her eyebrows, and Sissy sighed.

"Come downstairs, Harper. The party needs your attention now. You can give your attention to these boxes anytime."

Sissy turned and walked back toward the attic stairs.

Clasping the wooden box to her chest, Harper stood and surveyed the attic. If she'd been here, most of these items would have been donated. She wouldn't have kept it all. A lifetime sat in cardboard, overflowing into areas that could have been for other relatives. Her mother's lifetime reduced to cardboard boxes.

Every item her mother had owned at the time of her death, each holding a faded memory of a life cut short.

She would need to delve into each box and decide what memories she should keep.

Certainly not a task she wanted to tackle today.

Emmett

A cool breeze swept into the bar and ruffled the printed-paper napkins. The few midday patrons didn't flinch as they nestled their glasses and dipped their heads together in conversation. Emmett kicked his feet against the barstool and looked out toward the opened street view. The air smelled of alcohol and a strange herb. He'd certainly exited small town life for New Orleans, at least for a brief moment.

Edward Sawyer strolled in then, loosening his tie as he walked. Looking smart in his fitted gray suit, his slicked back hair managed to look professional even though it curled around the nape of his neck. Emmett could see the hint of the scar above his right eye where he'd hit the steering wheel going 118 miles an hour in an old Firebird he'd fixed up. They'd been in college—sophomore year. By law school, Sawyer had decided on different adventures—no less dangerous.

Sawyer nodded to the bartender as he slid onto the black stool next to Emmett. "Glad you could meet me here. My client was in the neighborhood, and I'm between meetings."

Emmett nursed his Sazerac, a drink he liked to order for the sound of it, not necessarily the taste. The strange combination of sweet and spice drew him every time though, at least when he drove into the city. "I was just glad you had time for me."

Sawyer smiled at the pretty bleach blonde who set the amber liquid down in front of him. Noticing the fake eyelashes dip, the bartender's brown eyes remained on his handsome friend. Sawyer had always attracted attention wherever they went, and his aloofness tended to drive the females crazy. "Of course, I can say I was surprised to get your call. It's been awhile."

Emmett stretched out in his seat, getting a feel for the people in the bar. It appeared to be mostly locals. "Law school seems like a long time ago. You've done well here."

"It's a living." Sawyer grinned. "It pays for my travels."

Emmett laughed. He hadn't changed much—always looking for the next adventure. In college, Emmett had admired that quality. He'd even believed he could have some of that life, but then he'd fallen into the family law firm and tried keeping it afloat. It had been like boarding a sinking ship and tossing the water out with a red Solo cup.

Emmett thumbed the swizzle stick in his cup. "I'm trying to make that kind of living. I'm considering antiquities law, and I've heard you know a thing or two about that area."

Sawyer nodded. "I do a little nonprofit, and I've handled a few cases."

"What's the work like?"

"I wouldn't call it an adventure. Lots of paperwork, but I do get to deal with art and antiquities. The truth is it's a difficult field to break into, not as muc work here as perhaps larger cities. I can't imagine there being much in your little small town."

Emmett felt a pinprick in that balloon of an idea and the air slowly deflated. As he'd brainstormed for a way to meld his childhood dream of treasure hunting with all these years of school and studies, he'd believed he'd found a path. He realized that it was unrealistic to try to recapture childhood goals, but he'd thought he could find some of that passion he'd had when he was a child.

Sawyer sipped from his glass and then grinned at him. "Law isn't what we thought it'd be, huh?"

The guy seemed happy. Always busy. Always somewhere to be. But then again, his social media accounts didn't include much about work. Perhaps he was just as disenchanted as Emmett.

"I'm currently out of the game," Emmett said, finally sipping from his glass, feeling the bitterness of the liquid swirl around his mouth.

Sawyer twiddled his fingers on the bar. "You know what I've learned?" He offered Emmett a sideways glance. "The job is just a job. It pays for my hobbies, and I work only enough to pay for what I really want to do. If I find myself working too many hours and I'm not enjoying life, then I cut back. I keep things simple."

Emmett nodded, thinking it over in his head. "Expensive hobbies?" He chuckled, thinking back to college days of sailing trips and of a brief motorcycle fad.

Sawyer shrugged. "What can I say? But seriously, you were always that dreamer. To tell you the truth, I was surprised you went to law school. But, you did it, so don't waste it. Use it to do whatever it is you really want to do. Branch out, find a hobby."

"Remember that trip to Mexico?"

Sawyer snorted, laughing hard. "How can I forget? We lost everything. Wallets, passports. Good thing we are good-looking and the border control agent was hot."

Emmett sipped at his drink again. "I haven't gone out of the country since then. I always thought I'd travel more."

When he was eight years old, he'd also thought he'd be turning up treasure every day—he knew better by the time he was twelve. He didn't mention this to his friend though; he didn't want to appear more pathetic than the unemployed person he was sure to appear to the easy-come lifestyle guy.

Sawyer downed the rest of his drink. "Can't go wrong with travel. It's a great hobby to have."

Everyone—Richard, Mr. Walter, Harper, Sawyer, his grandfather—seemed to have career advice to offer. His head swam with all the different ways he could fix this dissatisfaction with his life. Everyone had ideas except him. He had no idea what to do with all this advice.

He had to admit he liked the hobby idea though.

Harper

She'd made copious notes about the battle of Lafourche Crossing from the book her grandfather had given her to read. Details such as Union troops had abandoned Thibodaux and had moved to Lafourche Crossing to protect the railroad, a necessity for the troops to continue to move. On June 20, 1863, Confederate soldiers arrived- mostly Texas cavalry units—and surprised a skeleton Union crew in Thibodaux, causing them to escape toward Lafourche Crossing. The Confederates also seized the railroad depot in Shriever, sending those Union troops to Lafourche Crossing as well. When the battle was done 8 Union soldiers were dead and 41 wounded, while 53 Confederates were dead and 60 wounded.

All facts.

Granddaddy wanted her to find the story. So she'd read about the raining and the flooding—about the drunken ruckus on the battlefield as all the soldiers had drunk before heading off to battle. Bloody hand-to-hand combat. The wounded calling for water where they'd fallen. The killing of the chickens from the neighbors' farms for food.

She'd read details, but she didn't know if she'd grasped the story Granddaddy wanted.

Perhaps she needed a different book, or maybe there was something he'd forgotten to tell her. She didn't know what she should have discovered.

A soft knock sounded on her bedroom door. Glancing at the clock above the dresser, it read eleven o'clock. It could only be one person this late.

"Harper," Clint whispered from behind the door. "Can I come in a moment?"

Claiming her grandparents' old-fashioned principles, she'd shunted him into her uncle's room—the boy's room. He'd stayed away from her room until now.

Placing the book on the nightstand, she answered. "For a few minutes only."

Clint entered the room, soundlessly closing the door behind him. He surveyed the room. She looked around, wondering what he saw. The room hadn't changed since her mother was a girl. She and Sissy hadn't added much in terms of haphazard décor. The eclectic photographs scattered across the walls of everything from the Eiffel Tower to Buddha gave the room a fun, but disjointed vibe. Growing up, it had offered something of interest for both Sissy and Harper, so they hadn't wanted to change anything.

"I couldn't sleep," he announced, focusing his attention back on her. "I'm worried about us, this party, my exam in a few weeks. My mind won't stop. It's like that time when I didn't know if I'd get my internship."

Harper stared into his eyes, looking for some sign that he at least grasped the knowledge that she was the wrong person to talk to about this or anything at this moment in time. Perhaps somewhere between the bedroom down the hall and hers, the thought had occurred to him that he'd been responsible for the problems in his own life and it may not be a good idea to talk them through with the person he'd wronged.

Clint eased himself down onto the end of the mattress. "My parents want to come to the party."

Harper pulled her legs into her chest. "The party is a bad idea." He could have picked the other twin bed to sit on. It made the conversation too intimate, as if two friends were having a heart-to-heart. Weeks ago, this would have been the norm.

Clint frowned. "We can't cancel now. All our friends are coming. Our families. And I haven't given up on us either, but if we can't make it work, we can find a less public way to tell everyone we aren't getting married."

"People break up all the time."

"But what are you going to tell people?" he pleaded. She could smell his soap—a smell she'd always liked on him. "I don't want to break up. I want to live the life that I planned with my best friend."

Harper leaned back against the headboard. "What if I have different plans for my life?"

"Then, I won't take the job in North Carolina. I'll find something in the city, so you can finish your degree or write history books. Whatever it is you want to do. I'm so sorry I screwed up."

His shoulders drooped and the dark circles under his eyes deepened as he gazed expectantly at her. The sadness emanated from him in waves.

Harper inhaled deeply and exhaled slowly, providing herself

time to gather her thoughts. "I will hold off on making a decision until after the party in a week. In the meantime, go to sleep. You have an hour drive to the city tomorrow for your shift."

He stood and stretched his neck back and then side-to-side before he smiled. "I'm going to convince you, Harper Ames."

Harper resisted the urge to roll her eyes. Clint needed direction right now, and she was struggling not to show him the way to the door.

Slipping out the door as quietly as he entered, Clint exited more confident than when he'd entered minutes ago.

Picking up her powered off cell phone, she turned it on and dialed Tara.

A sleepy, muffled voice answered the phone.

Harper pictured Tara's springy curls splayed wildly across her white sheets with her eyes closed as she felt around for her phone. Predictability was one of the woman's strong traits.

"Tara," Harper said, "I need to see you in person."

"Girl," a much more alert voice than expected responded, "I get some cryptic message about you not being able to shop for a dress because Clint cheated on you not to mention a tangent about a sick grandpa, and then I hear from Lisa that there is an engagement party and you haven't returned any of my four hundred calls. Why am I dropping everything and coming to see you again?"

Harper swallowed against the nausea gurgling in her throat. "I'm having an engagement party because Clint doesn't want anyone to know that we aren't getting married. I caught him cheating on me with Felipe."

Silence echoed from the other side of the line.

"I'll be there tomorrow morning."

Emmett

Between his grandfather's recent conversation and Sawyer's career advice, he'd spent a sleepless night agonizing over his next move. He couldn't handle inaction, so he knew he needed to do something to proceed. After two hours of fitful sleep, he knew he'd start with his mother and move on to his career once that situation was resolved. For peace of mind, he needed to know what had happened back then. On one hand, he wanted to know if he'd shut his mother out all these years for something she couldn't control, but on the other hand, he was thirty-years old and she could have told him the truth at any point since childhood. However, if money had been exchanged, she didn't fare any better than Winston. Once all of the details were clear, he was sure he could get his head straight and back to job worries.

On the way to his sedan, he spotted Mr. Walter wandering around the field, chickens pecking the ground all around him. No one else appeared to be outside. He wondered if Mrs. Patsy knew the man's whereabouts.

Passing up his car, he strolled toward Mr. Walter, hoping today was a day that the old man remembered who he was.

Sometimes the man expected Emmett to be a little boy, which Emmett imagined would make life tremendously easier.

Emmett approached slowly as not to startle him. "Mr. Walter, are you out feeding the chickens this morning?"

Walter grinned, pausing in his circling pace. "Ah, so you know me? I think I'm taking a walk. Aren't the chickens lovely?"

"Yes." Emmett peered off towards the house. No one was coming. He couldn't even see Mrs. Patsy at her usual seat by the windows, a seat she occupied whenever the man took to working in the yard. "Would you like to walk back inside now?"

Mr. Walter rubbed his hand across his perspiring forehead, the sun already glaring down early this morning. "I was looking for something, but I can't seem to remember what it is now. My memory's not working quite like it used to be, I suppose. Be thankful for your youth, young man." He glanced at him sideways. "I'm sorry, I didn't get your name."

With his arm, Emmett gestured toward the big house so that Mr. Walter would begin walking in that direction. "Emmett, sir."

"The neighbor's little boy is named Emmett. He's friends with my granddaughters." Mr. Walter bobbed his head. "Good boy."

"That's me, Mr. Walter," Emmett said. "We're all grown up now."

"Of course, I knew that," Mr. Walter said, taking a tentative step forward. A look of confusion crinkled his forehead. "Have you seen my granddaughter?"

"She's visiting right now," Emmett said, matching his pace to Mr. Walter's slow stumble. "She may be inside."

"Good, good." He looked up. "I do remember you, you know? You gave your grandmother a run for her money. She has a hard time keeping up with you." He chuckled, leaning on Emmett's shoulder as his knee gave out. "You keep her young though."

Emmett smiled. The ache in his chest a little less with each mention of his grammy, even though it was obvious that in this moment Mr. Walter could not remember that she was gone. As a rambunctious child, Emmett had kept his grandmother busy with patching the knees of his pants and bandaging the scrapes on his elbows. As an adult, he hoped she'd loved him no matter how rough he'd made the time she should have been able to relax after her own child was raised.

Mr. Walter looked out over his home, the lines on his forehead crinkled deeper. Emmett imagined the old man felt like it was twenty years ago and didn't understand the changes that had occurred in that time. His memories of the past seemed more concrete than the present. This gave Emmett an idea. "What do you remember about my mother?"

"Bad business, that." Mr. Walter's knuckles shook as he reached out to steady himself on Emmett's shoulder. "A mother should always have their child if they want him. Your grandmother thought so."

Emmett remained quiet as they took the final steps towards the back porch. By this time, the back door had flown open and Harper came hurrying out to meet them.

"Thank you, Emmett," she said, frenzied. "Tara arrived from the city, and it took us several minutes to realize he'd slipped out of the house."

"No problem," Emmett said. "He's good company."

"Harper?" Mr. Walter questioned, squinting at her as if he was trying to make sense of her face.

Even with her hair whipping wildly about and her face free of makeup except for that raspberry lip stain he'd noticed she always wore now, she looked stunning. At least Emmett thought so.

Harper slipped her arm through Mr. Walter's. "Granddaddy, I have someone for you to meet. You will love her because she works at the history museum."

"Really?" Mr. Walter's interest piqued.

"You can tell her about the family treasure."

"Fascinating," he said, focusing on the porch. "Perhaps she'd enjoy the store as well."

Harper's eyes met Emmett's then, open and searching. It was as if she needed to tell him something, but he didn't understand what she was trying to convey. He wished he could get the message, but it was still off limits for him to ask.

"Thank you again, Emmett," she said. "Grams made fruit tarts if you'd like one. I would love it if you'd eat the rest so I'd stop shoveling them down."

He laughed. "I'm on the way to see my mother. I kind of need to get it over with before I lose my nerve."

"Umm." Her eyes pierced through him. "How about you come over later for a fruit tart and tell me all about it."

He nodded. "Depending on what I hear, I may need Scotch."

Mr. Walter coughed, staring above Emmett's head. "I have a bottle from 1968. I think it's time to open it and taste it."

Harper nodded at him, her eyes still on his. "I'll have the glass waiting."

With her reassuring words in his head, he carried himself to his car, and the car carried him to the baseball field where his mother could be found most days of the week with his teenage half brothers. When he'd called to speak to her, she'd told him she'd already volunteered to restock the concession stand this morning for tonight's game. Not wanting to lose momentum, he'd decided to seek her out at the field.

Only three cars were parked outside the stadium, and Emmett found the concession stand box easily. He could hear noise from within, but the door was closed and wouldn't budge when he pulled the makeshift handle.

He knocked and no one came. He knocked louder and the top of the door swung open towards him. He stepped quickly out of the way to miss being hit by the heavy plywood.

A petite blonde stared at him with wide-set blue eyes. "Can I help you?"

"I'm looking for Toni?"

"It's okay, Hope." She came from behind holding a large box of chocolate candy. "This is my son."

"Oh." Hope smiled as she tilted her chin to the side. "Didn't realize you had one that wasn't a teenager."

"Watch it now." His mother smiled. "That's my boy."

Emmett awkwardly fidgeted. "I was hoping we could speak for a moment."

"Of course," she said, a frown tugging at the corner of her lips. "I'll step out for a moment, and we can sit in the bleachers."

Glancing back, Emmett saw the metal bleachers overlooking the empty field and nodded.

He strolled over in that direction and sank onto the

uncomfortable, squeaking bleachers and waited for her to let herself out, wipe her hands on her jeans, and walk towards him. She looked concerned, unsure of herself. To tell the truth, it was a look she wore most of the time when they had encounters. Having missed all those bonding years, neither of them knew a comfortable space to ease into when confronted with a simple conversation.

She sat down next to him, leaving five feet between them. He'd set these parameters when he'd been young, and she'd followed them since. Neither had broken the habit, and he'd never questioned it until now.

She folded her hands in her lap. "What's up?"

"Winston and the Judge told me that you didn't give me up, that the Judge forced you to do it." He swallowed as he watched her eyes immediately water and her face screw up. "I want to hear your side of the story."

"Why?" She choked on the word, cleared her throat, and tried again. "Why did they tell you that now?"

Emmett looked out over the field, the red dirt all in neat lines—perfectly straight and formed for the game. The coach had good intentions, but the players would destroy the lines and kick up dust everywhere. Just like people did with life. Why had Winston told him now? It wasn't like Winston to do anything but give him a hard time and push his buttons, but this had been different. "I think Winston wants me to give you a second chance."

Taking a haggard breath, she straightened out her trembling fingers against her pant's leg. "Winston cheated on me after I got pregnant. He's not exactly reliable, but I should have known that before I became involved with him. He could be charming, though, and sometimes he could be real with me. Pregnant and rejected, senior year of high school was miserable, but then I got a scholarship to the University of Alabama. You and I could have had a fresh start. He planned to go to LSU anyway. We'd both be away at college."

He nodded, hoping to encourage her without speaking.

"Your grandfather got wind of my plans and approached me, offered to pay me to leave you behind."

Emmett's gut tightened. "You took money?"

She shook her head, her short hair bouncing around. "It didn't matter though. In the end, he had you taken away from me legally by proving me an unfit mother." She heaved against a few sobs before pulling herself together, straightening her shoulders. "I got caught with Winston's drug stash in my car because he'd put it in your diaper bag. Your grandfather knew it belonged to Winston, but he could get what he wanted and not ruin his son's life all at the same time."

His grandfather had fixed it. Winston had said this to him. He glanced down at her, her knuckles white from the squeezing of her knees. "You didn't go to Alabama."

A tear slipped down her cheek. "I lost my scholarship over the arrest. Besides, I couldn't go that far from you, especially when your grandmother would allow me to see you sometimes."

"Why didn't you ever tell me?"

She smiled at him through watery eyes. "Making you hate your grandfather or your father wouldn't have made you a better person. Besides, I don't think your grandfather is a terrible person. He believes he is taking care of his son, no matter how misguided his intentions. Sometimes parents can't see the clear picture when it comes to their children. Winston's chances in life have suffered because your grandfather can't see clearly. And that means they deserve some sympathy, no matter how difficult that may be for me to admit some days."

Frustration welled inside of Emmett. He should have known all of this before he was thirty years old. He'd shut this woman out for abandoning him, and she hadn't. He'd admired his grandparents for taking him in when he'd been abandoned by his parents, but they'd deprived him of his mother.

Everything he'd believed had been the truth about his family had been a lie.

Harper

Tara threw herself across the opposite twin bed. "Your grandfather is cool for an old man."

Harper sat down, pulling the pillow into her middle. "I just wish he'd have all his memories. Dementia sucks."

Tara nodded vigorously up and down. "Okay, girl, tell me. I've waited patiently for hours. What is going on?"

Harper pulled the pillow to her face, wishing it was as easy to smother the memories of the last few weeks as it was to cut off her breath with the darkness. "I should have told my grandparents when I first arrived that the wedding was off. None of this would be happening if I had."

Harper chewed on her bottom lip, considering how she could have changed the outcome by simply admitting the truth from the beginning. Wasn't there a verse about "the pride cometh before the fall"? She'd been so determined to save face in front of Sissy that she hadn't thought the consequences through. Maybe it would be nice to have selective dementia—to choose what memories you lose.

"But Felipe?" Tara exclaimed, sitting up and facing her. "He walks gay pride parades, has calendars of firemen in his office, has better nails than I do. Why would he be willing to hide a relationship with Clint?"

"Who knows? It doesn't matter now, does it?" Harper said, tossing the pillow across the room at the door. "Ugh! I need to figure out what to do with my life."

Tara stood, her pantsuit unwrinkled by the drive or the bed. "You need a plan. Party or not, you can't hide out here for the rest of your life."

Harper leaned back against the headboard. "Why not? I like it here."

Tara glared at her, the smoky eyes clouding. "I didn't see a coffee shop anywhere near here or a building over two stories for that matter."

Harper shrugged. "My cousin owns a café. It's next door to the antique store that I will inherit."

"Inherit?" Tara raised an eyebrow. "You mean, I will have to continue driving here to see my best friend?"

"I don't know. How am I supposed to know what I'm going to do with my life?" Harper threw her hands in the air. "A week ago I had a plan. Get married when Clint finished his internship in a few weeks and pack everything and move wherever he took a job. Distantly, I had a degree I wanted to finish, but that was like a wish list."

Harper pulled another pillow and shoved it against her face and inhaled. It smelled of dryer sheets and lavender.

"Okay," Tara said, "we can work with this."

Tara paced the room, her pumps making a cushioned thump against the floorboards as she walked. She moved her hands to the rhythm of her thoughts. "Do you want to tell your grandparents the wedding is off?"

Harper squeezed her hands, considering how much Grams would be disappointed. "I just don't want to be a failure."

"You are not a failure," Tara said forcefully in her take-charge voice. "Shit happens, and let's be frank, Clint shit all over this one."

Harper giggled, the sound bubbling up. Tara's forehead remained furrowed with her deep thoughts.

"I say you stay here and finish your dissertation. Well, write a new one because we both know the other one was crap because you were distracted by new love." Tara raised her eyebrows, looking her in the eyes, daring her to argue.

Harper raised her own eyebrow in response and nodded. They'd begun their doctorates together, and Tara had reamed her when she'd sat out, even offering her opinion of the offensive writing piece at the time. Harper had heard all of this before, only in nicer terms.

"If you want to tell your grandparents now, tell them. If you want to wait, you can say the long distance killed the relationship. Or perhaps that good looking gentleman from this morning will have stepped in and be the reason."

Harper shook her head. "And you were doing so well."

"What?" Tara said. "Your grams mentioned he's a neighbor. The hot neighbor next door. Who can blame you for moving on with options like that?"

"There's history there," Harper said. "You know why we study history?"

"Bullshit," Tara said, smiling, her eyes twinkling. "We make the same mistakes all the time. When a hot man's involved, at least it can be fun."

Harper laughed. "Why are you still single?"

"Opinions are like a handkerchief," Tara said. "A man always has one and wants to give it away to a lady. I'm not very good at accepting."

Harper chuckled.

Emmett

Harper grabbed the bottle of Scotch from him in one hand, gripping the shovel in the other. Dancing around the shovel's handle, she took a swig from the bottle and then held it out for Emmett.

"You know," she said, stopping suddenly. "I don't think my granddaddy will ever find this treasure."

"It is a long shot," Emmett said, taking his own sip, feeling it burn the back of his throat. His esophagus and internal organs should be numb with as much as they'd drunk, but unfortunately he continued to feel as it slid down.

"I mean what if Ellis lied and actually dug it up and kept it all for himself?" she said, leaning her chin on the handle. "Or some other family member discovered it in the last one hundred fifty years?"

He grinned. "All possibilities."

They'd been digging for the last hour by lantern and the beam of a flashlight. It had begun in the study with a toast by Mr. Walter, and in some zigzag path of conversation, he and Harper had pilfered the bottle of Scotch and located the shovels in the old barn and begun digging in Mr. Walter's carefully chosen next spot.

She grinned. "I should have been a treasure hunter." All of the tension had disappeared from her face, and she looked almost fifteen again. Almost the Harper he'd known before all her tragedy.

"When you were eight, that was your intention." He shone the light on the growing holes around the backside of the chicken coop. In fright, the chickens had retreated from the activity, escaping into their multistoried coop.

"I settled for wanting to be a history professor." She frowned, twisting the corner of her mouth. "But I didn't finish that either."

"It's not too late," he said, hoping to return her smile.

She smiled. It didn't quite reach her eyes this time though. "What about you? You wanted to be an adventurer. Explore the world. An eight year old who wanted to climb Mount Everest or swim in the Atlantic Ocean."

He laughed, thinking about that passport in a box somewhere he'd used only once for that trip to Mexico. "I haven't done either. Law school drained my ambition."

"What happened to us?" she asked, scrunching up her button nose. "We turned into boring adults."

"Our parents," he muttered. "Let's blame it on our parents like every other sensible adult in our generation."

Her expression became thoughtful as she looked at him, unencumbered because of the Scotch. "I've been thinking about your story since you told me. I think they all hold blame, you know what I mean? I can't imagine my mother not fighting for me. When my dad left, she told him he could visit whenever he wanted, but she'd never gone a day without seeing me, and she didn't plan to start now."

Harper looked toward her old house, as if she could imagine the conversation happening. Emmett could imagine Beth Ames saying that to Mr. Curtis. The woman had been fierce. Harper shared many features with her mother, except for her father's dark hair. But even still, she had those blonde streaks like her mother's hair. There wasn't a part of Harper that her mother hadn't touched in some way.

"I don't think my mother was as strong as your mama," he said, picturing Ms. Beth standing in the front of the old house, a bandana holding back yards of hair, with that button nose like Harper's flaring in anger. When they'd built a labyrinth in the yard and destroyed gallons of her paint for a house she'd been working on, he'd witnessed the fierceness firsthand. His mother would have only cried in the middle of the mess.

"True." Harper nodded. "And the Judge is no pushover. More of a Doberman."

Emmett reached for the shovel to occupy his frustration. "I should have seen this coming. I should have asked questions, something."

"Don't beat yourself up about it," she said, taking a sip from the bottle. "I think everyone is just bumping along doing the best they can, making mistakes as they go."

While she studied Mr. Walter's sketch with the flashlight, he thought about what she'd said. Had she forgiven him for his mistake then? They'd never had the conversation, and when he'd tried to bring it up the other day, she'd brushed it aside.

But he needed to know. Maybe it was the Scotch talking, but they were outside on an adventure like old times. It must mean that there was hope for the two of them to move past all the bad things that had happened.

"I've always felt like I could have changed the night your mother died," he said, struggling with how to ask for her forgiveness.

Her face popped up from the schematic.

He felt the Scotch burning at the back of his throat. "You know Winston and I argued that day, and I told him he was the worst father in the world and a bunch of other things I don't remember now."

"Emmett..." Harper said.

"I'm sure he was drinking that day because of the argument. He was out of his mind when he walked back to the front from crashing the car. Didn't even remember driving."

"Don't..."

"That day I'd told you about the argument, and you'd made me feel better. But then I found out what happened, and we didn't get to speak. My grandfather wouldn't allow me to go to the funeral because of the lawyer's advice, and when I finally could get away to see you, your father had taken you away. I couldn't apologize and tell you I wished I could take it back."

"Stop," Harper said, holding her hand out as if she needed to physically push his words away. "We can't relive it. *I can't relive it.*"

He moved in closer to her, the Scotch providing liquid courage. "I've really missed you, Harper. There's not a memory from my childhood that doesn't involve you, and they were happy memories. I'm so sorry for everything."

She stepped back from him. "Emmett, you want some kind of forgiveness that I can't offer you."

He swallowed against the bile rising in his throat. "Why?"

"It's not your fault my mother died," she said, blinking against tears. "Your father got trashed at least three times a week. You don't even know if he was drinking because of you or just because he's Winston."

He exhaled, feeling relief begin to ease the strain in his shoulders. "So you don't blame me?"

"Not for my mother's death." She looked at him, deep into his eyes. "You never tried to reach out to me though. Ever. Even after the night that I showed up devastated that your father would never have a consequence. Nothing. We'd seen each other every day our entire lives, and you didn't try to be there for me in the most painful moment of my life."

Under the lantern light, the pain dulled her green eyes. Her disappointment jabbed at him.

She bit down on her bottom lip. "I think we should continue digging tomorrow."

A thin form walked around the chicken wire fence, and Sissy's face became clear as she reached the line of the lantern glow.

She hissed. "What are you two doing?"

Harper stepped backwards towards the house. "We're finished for tonight."

Sissy looked from Emmett to Harper. "Isn't it enough that Granddaddy is destroying the yard? Why are you encouraging him?"

Harper turned away. "Good night, Sissy."

Sissy turned on him, her eyes accusing him as well. "Did I interrupt something?"

Emmett tossed the Scotch bottle into the hole, wondering how they could all be so alienated after their closeness as children. Growing up, he'd believed this would be his family, that they'd figure out all the answers of life together. But today they couldn't figure out how to be in the same room for ten minutes without finding a way to hurt each other. He didn't know how to put those pieces together.

He'd have to erase the past. And that he didn't know how to do.

Harper

The bell jangled their arrival at Ames Antiques, and Harper resisted yanking it from its metal bracket. Busy scanning the shop with his critical eagle eye, Granddaddy didn't seem to notice the jarring noise. Perhaps her reaction had more to do with the Scotch headache than the bell. She didn't know what she had been thinking last night.

Granddaddy mumbled, "Too much merchandise crowding the front displays." He wasn't speaking to her, as momentarily he seemed to have forgotten she was in the shop beside him.

At breakfast, he'd been adamant about visiting the store today. Yesterday he'd experienced confusion much of the day, but today he'd appeared lucid. Grams had confided that she thought it was time to call the doctor and question his medication. Harper agreed.

Now, he walked and stood in front of a display case of random, cluttered items. Searching for the fake vase, Harper found it after a moment hidden on a different shelf among other mismatched items. The Hummel still collected dust on the shelf in the same spot, as if it hadn't been touched since she'd picked it up.

Granddaddy looked at her, his bushy eyebrows meeting at the bridge of his nose. "Harper, today must be cleaning day."

Harper nodded, not wanting to disappoint him with the truth. Her warning of her granddaddy's upcoming visit had brought no changes in the lazy Albert.

The culprit slinked from the back room, his glasses dangling from his nose, a book held in both hands. "Can I help…?"

Albert glanced up at them and his bottom lip fell, aghast.

Granddaddy squared his shoulders and raised his voice so that it filled the customerless shop. "Albert, old scalawag, I hear you have taken over my shop."

A smile twisted at Albert's lips, one that didn't erase the strain around his eyes. "Sissy felt I was the best person for the job."

Granddaddy grunted and walked around the chaotic display case, his eyes absorbing every detail. "Then what kind of profit is the shop turning?"

Albert shook his head. "Sissy controls the books."

Granddaddy's voice boomed. "But you know how sales have been, old man."

Albert stared at him unresponsive. Harper almost felt sorry for him. Almost.

Granddaddy lumbered toward the back display cases. "No matter. Today I want to show my granddaughter something."

Within these enclosed glass cases sat the antique jewelry, which typically went for the long sale. Once, he'd told her that he'd priced the items so that the buyer appreciated the story behind the piece—a story he made sure he knew about each item he collected for the shop.

Trailing behind him, Harper inhaled the muskiness of the old items around her with the flittering of dust particles floating in the air to be inhaled as she walked.

As he leaned over the glass case, she looked around at a few familiar vestiges of her many hours spent here. An old 1920s typewriter still rested in a display case with a not so old copy of an Ernest Hemingway novel. An old travel trunk from the late 1800s was shoved against the back wall and loaded down with a box of old vintage albums. Albert probably didn't realize that the trunk was an actual antique and not just a storage vessel. Many items her granddaddy would have never housed in his time running the shop overcrowded the place now.

It needed a thorough cleaning.

Granddaddy's voice boomed toward Albert. "Where is it?"

Harper turned back toward the display case to look into the depths of broaches and rings and even a delicate hair comb with ruby encrusted droplets.

Albert shuffled toward them, alarmed. "Where's what?"

Granddaddy's head bobbed back and forth as he looked in every crevice of the glass. "My mother's ring."

Blood rushed through her ears. Her great grandmother's ring had been her own mother's wedding ring: passed down through the family in a succession of inherited objects – the one missing from her mother's collection, missing from the box that now sat in her room.

Albert beamed. "It sold. A very fine price I was told."

Granddaddy pounded his fist down on the display. "It wasn't for sale." The jewelry rattled. "It had a sign that said not for sale."

She'd only ever seen her granddaddy angry once and that was when the police stood in the living room and delivered the truth of her mother's death, after Winston Hebert had been forced to admit he'd been joy riding through the fields. Of course, he didn't remember running her over and leaving her to die from internal bleeding two hours later as she lay in the field unconscious. Their investigation had revealed those details, and Granddaddy had tossed an antique lamp at a wall in response.

Albert withdrew, clutching his book to his chest. "I wasn't responsible for the sale. Sissy told me of its transaction when I returned from a bout of the flu."

Sissy. Of course, she'd have something to do with it.

Harper felt an anger clamping down tightly against her ribs and squeezing.

Granddaddy turned towards her, his eyes welling with unshed tears. "I wanted you to have it. I noticed you weren't wearing a ring."

She pulled at her bare fingers. "Clint said he'd buy me one when he could afford it."

Truthfully, at the time, she'd been hurt that he couldn't have simply bought something small. She didn't care for an extravagant, oversized diamond. She'd assured him it was okay though, not to hurt his feelings. But what she'd come to understand is that Clint wanted flashy, something to show off, or nothing at all. He had the patience to wait so he could tell everyone to look at what he'd bought. She could despise him for it, but she knew he'd grown up poor in an affluent neighborhood. It had given him a complex.

But her mother's ring had always been her idea of a wedding ring. When her mother had died, Harper believed the ring returned to the family since it was a family heirloom—one of only a few not buried somewhere in an unknown location. Now that she knew the ring could have been hers, she found the anger suffocating.

"Everything's changing Harper." Granddaddy's eyes crinkled at the corners into deep crevices. "It's hard for my memory to hold on to things."

Her anger dissipated, replaced by an aching. "Some things will always stay the same." She leaned into him, offering him comfort, which he embraced and leaned back into her. "I will always be your favorite."

He chuckled, blinking away his unshed tears.

"You and me are going to find that treasure." He put his arm around her and squeezed. "They are going to write an article about us."

Her chest ached. She didn't know how that would happen, but she didn't care if he dug up the entire yard looking until he couldn't remember that he was looking for the treasure anymore.

Albert cleared his throat. "Will you be doing the showing for the person who's going to lease out the second floor?"

Harper narrowed her eyes at the incompetent, small man. She didn't know what Albert was talking about, and she was positive no one had sent her granddaddy with the responsibility of that task.

Emmett

Tossing and turning and unable to rest his mind, his thoughts had run over all the chaos of his life. In the midst of his racing thoughts, he'd drifted to sleep, only to wake up feverish at 4 A.M. with the onslaught of an idea. He'd lain among the strange pillows, staring up at the ceiling—the only thing familiar in the room that had been his growing up—allowing his idea to fully form and work the kinks out. By the time he arose from bed at seven, he'd been ready to sell Sissy on the idea.

She hadn't needed much selling. She'd agreed to meet him above Ames Antique's after he met with his financial advisor. The gray-haired financial advisor had mumbled about forms and about how Grammy had never been this much trouble.

Sissy clacked around the wooden floors. "We'd need to do something with those stairs, of course."

Emmett nodded, too busy scanning the area making a mental list of the work that would have to be done to make it a presentable place. The upstairs of the Ames building hadn't been used for anything but storage in the last thirty years.

"The back area is still used as storage for the antique shop," she rattled on. "If you need the space, I can see what we can do. It's probably all trash anyway."

He could imagine a desk right in front of the windows where he could stare out over the street. Too bad it didn't have a balcony, but he could open the windows and allow the breeze to blow through and breathe the fresh air. He'd need to do something with the horrible paneling and broken molding so the inside didn't make him want to spend too much time dreaming about what lay outside of the these walls.

Sissy leaned against a thick doorway, a signature piece of architecture of this place. "I'm so proud of you for doing this."

He ran his hand along the window seal. Old windows, but the seals felt tight. "I need to do something."

She stepped closer. "That's how I felt when I opened the café. Everything had been decided for me up until that point, but I needed to have something I'd created for myself. And look how well that turned out."

Emmett glanced back at her as she stood in the middle of the empty room. With her jeans and button down shirt, she looked like the young girl he'd grown up with, only vulnerable instead of mean.

"You know," he picked through his words carefully, "I think if you called a truce with Harper, you may get to have your life back. She could help you out."

She smiled demurely, her eyes narrowing. "I don't know what you mean, Emmett Hebert. I'm throwing my dear cousin an engagement party."

He nodded with a smile. "I haven't figured that one out yet, but I know you'd love to move back into your apartment, so a real truce may be worth it."

She sighed. "I'm leasing it out right now, but Harper's getting married and moving away, so that would only be wishful thinking on my part."

Emmett sensed something going on with Harper and didn't think she'd be moving so soon, but he didn't want to irritate Sissy. Her moods were swift, and right now it was in his favor.

"Anyway," he said, looking up at the wood plank ceiling. "I think it's worth a shot, but I'm going to take this place. It needs some work, but I need something to do with myself so it's perfect."

She clapped her hands together. "Fantastic, I will have the lawyer send over the lease agreement today. You can begin whenever you like though. I'll let Albert know that you will be working up here so he doesn't have a heart attack."

Harper stood in the doorway, hand on hip. "What exactly are we doing in my building?"

Neither of them had heard her come up the rickety stairs. Emmett couldn't help but feel the excitement tremble through him as he drank in her skintight jeans and silky hair, but then the intensity of her glare registered and he knew trouble brewed.

Sissy's face scrunched into a scowl. "This isn't your building. I'm the building manager, and I'm leasing the second floor to Emmett as office space, if you must know."

"You *were* building manager," Harper said. "I've decided to take over now. I don't appreciate how poorly my inheritance is being managed."

Sissy crossed her arms across her chest. "How ridiculous. You're getting married, and Clint has no intentions of living here. He told me so himself."

"I've decided to stay here to finish my doctorate. Perhaps I can get things straight in the meantime. At least I won't sell our great grandmother's ring and break our granddaddy's heart."

Harper and Sissy stared at each other, neither blinking.

"I brought him home devastated, in case you want to know. I suppose you hoped he wouldn't remember the ring and that he wanted me to have it."

The tension in the air felt as if it crackled against the old walls. Emmett felt as though the plaster might crumble under the strain.

"Ladies." He cleared his throat, not even certain he wanted to attempt to mediate this one. He was considering ducking out and leaving them to it. In the interest of self-preservation, that might be the best idea.

"It's always about you, right?" Sissy said, softly, shaking her head. "I have to get back to the café. We'll talk later, Emmett."

Putting her head down and hunching her shoulders, Sissy disappeared around the bend of the stairs. Emmett noticed a few tears escape before she tucked her head down closer to her chest.

"Harper," he said. "I'm not saying she's right, but I wish you two would just talk. It hasn't been easy for her."

Harper glared at him. "Right. Both her parents are alive and give her everything she wants while she lives for free in my mother's house. How exactly has her life been tough?"

Judging from her anger, it was no use to try and reason with her right now. Why had Sissy gone and sold that ring? He could have stood a chance with this plan he'd cooked up in the few hours of sleep—all three of them working together as they'd done as children. Times had been good then. Just a moment ago, he'd thought he was on his way to this vision he had in his head. Now, it seemed more adrift.

"That's what I thought." She'd assumed his silence meant agreement instead of his inability to reason with her when she was angry. "However, I don't have an issue with you leasing this floor. It will give me some income to make some changes with the shop not doing well."

"Are you going to stay?"

She looked at him, almost through him, and turned and retreated down the stairs.

He released a breath he didn't know he was holding.

Harper

She'd been furious with Sissy, but now she was furious with herself. Driving her granddaddy home, she'd half-heartedly attempted to convince herself that she should wait to confront Sissy when she'd calmed down and had gathered more facts. But her internal monologue had been useless against Granddaddy's sad eyes and stooped shoulders as he'd shuffled to his bedroom, claiming he needed a nap.

Assuring herself that she could hold a civil conversation had been a lie.

Parking among the many cars in what looked like a parking lot at her grandparents' house, she exhaled and loosened her grip on the steering wheel. She'd hoped to slip in unnoticed before Grams's quilting group roamed the house. Perhaps if she were lucky, she could still go unnoticed and make it to her room for a moment of quiet, only Clint was driving in from his shift in the city any moment. It had been such a relief for him to be gone, even though she had more than enough other issues to deal with since he'd returned to the city for his rotation.

Easing in through the back door, she peeked her head in and

looked around for any of the ladies. Before her a table was laden with mismatched dishes, likely all brought by the different women, but no one occupied the kitchen area presently.

She gently closed the door and turned to walk lightly toward the stairs when a tiny, white-haired lady entered the room. A loud rumble of laughter trickled in from the front room.

The white-haired woman smiled as she picked up a small paper plate. "I don't blame you, dear, for sneaking in. We make more noise than quilts."

Harper stopped, unsure how rude it would be to continue her scramble to the stairs. "I didn't want to interrupt."

"Nonsense." An orange-haired woman glided in wearing a white pants suit. The contrasting colors were shocking. "Fresh blood to the mix is always welcome."

"Nadia." The white-haired woman had a warning in her voice even though she continued serving a plate without interruption.

Nadia clicked her tongue. "I believe this is the one getting married soon. I'm sure she has all sorts of fascinating tales to tell."

"Nothing like that," Harper said quickly. She did not want to get roped into telling stories of how she and Clint met or how he proposed, all tales people typically wanted to hear. She couldn't say they were romantic tales. More like sweet, and certainly not something she wanted to think about when she was struggling to imagine a future completely different than her last six years.

"Honey pie," Nadia said, tilting her head back, sassy-like. "You need to make the stories when you're young. Don't wait until you're old like us. Then it may be too late."

"Take that with a grain of salt." White-haired woman shook

her head in disapproval. "She's been married four times."

"I enjoyed my life." Nadia scowled, and then gestured with both her hands upwards to indicate she didn't understand. "Which is more than I can say for most."

Grams floated in, a gauzy, purple-flowered number floating around her. "Nadia, please don't try to influence my granddaughter."

"Pish." Nadia threw her arms up dramatically. "You could do worse, Child."

Harper laughed.

"Debra needs some help with those stitches." Grams stirred in one of the dishes with a silver-serving spoon. "I'm pretty sure she needs new glasses."

The women laughed as they exited the room, discussing Debra and her inability to keep track of her bifocals.

Grams rested the spoon on the side of the dish and looked at her, eyes intense. "You spoke to Sissy at the shop?"

Harper nodded. "It didn't go well. I don't remember when we started hating each other. I think maybe it was junior high when she became friends with all those popular girls that wore pink and were hideous people."

Grams frowned. "You two are different, but very much alike. You need to figure out a way to get back to a place where you remember that."

Normally, Harper didn't disagree with Grams, but she didn't understand how she and Sissy were alike. Even as children, they'd been opposite, but back then they'd managed to make it work somehow. Selling the ring felt unforgivable though. It had been a family heirloom, but it had also been representative of

Harper's parents—when they'd loved each other and could make their marriage work. How could Sissy have sold it and thought it would be okay? Harper couldn't understand what could have made her think that the family would not have a reaction to this.

Grams shuffled toward the back window. "Your granddaddy has decided to find the treasure. Says he's sure that there will be another ring inside for you to wear."

Harper groaned.

Grams turned. "You don't want a ring?"

Harper felt the piercing of her grandmother's faded green eyes. "It's not that." She didn't want her grandparents to think she didn't appreciate the effort, although she didn't believe it was possible to find the family heirlooms.

Grams reached out and brushed her arm. "What is it then?"

Harper buckled. Now would be the time to come clean and get it all out. "Clint and I are having issues… well, one big issue right now."

Grams moved toward the window. "Problems are normal, especially when trying to make wedding plans."

"Not this kind of issue," Harper mumbled, wondering what her grandparents thought about homosexuality. They did belong to a different generation. Clint's parents were older. His mother had been 44 at his birth. Did he fear their disapproval? Is that what his denial was about? Harper really shouldn't waste time analyzing Clint, unless she'd decided to forgive him. She didn't have an answer for that question of herself either.

"What, dear?"

"I've decided to stay here and finish my dissertation while Clint figures out his career plans."

Grams glanced back with sharp eyes. "Do you think living long distance is a good idea?"

"At this point, a very good idea." Harper didn't blink and Grams's eyes sparked.

For a moment, Harper recognized some of the old fire there, as if her grams had some devious plan in mind. The woman glanced back out the window, so Harper couldn't say if she imagined it or not.

Grams gasped.

Harper crossed quickly to where the woman stared out the window, her hand covering her mouth.

Through the glass, she saw her granddaddy struggling with the Judge, the shovel between them.

Emmett

As Emmett pulled into the back garage, the mounting pile of clippings and weeds caught his attention. Around the courtyard, the overgrown shrubbery looked cleaner, as if it held a shape instead of the gnarled and tangled mass it had been days ago when he'd last did some trimming.

Since his grandfather hadn't hired anyone, the only logical answer was that Winston had continued working. That the man would do manual labor—something he'd always felt was beneath him—was a sign of something underfoot. Emmett may need to check up on whether Winston had joined a cult or had undergone hypnosis recently. He certainly hadn't checked into a rehab facility.

After shutting off the engine, he stepped out of his car and heard the first yell. He pivoted toward the sound but couldn't see anything among the trees and shrubbery bordering the property.

Another yell pierced the peaceful midafternoon heat.

He took off at a jog in that direction. As soon as he cleared the row of camellia bushes, he happened upon his grandfather and Mr. Walter struggling to maintain their grip on a yellow-handled shovel. Harper had her arms splayed out attempting to keep them apart with no affect.

He leapt in and grabbed his grandfather by the shoulder, soft tissue filling his hands. Harper, seeing the help, changed tactics and stood in front of Mr. Walter and pushed him backwards with her body.

Harper huffed. "You two need to stop. One of you will get hurt and five feet of property won't be worth it."

Emmett felt his grandfather tug against his grip. "Judge."

The Judge yanked his shoulder forward. "It's worth it."

The man was stubborn. Squeezing down on his grandfather's thick, swollen knuckles clasping the shovel, Emmett wrapped his own hand around his grandfather's hand and pulled back.

The release of friction propelled the other two backwards, and Emmett could only watch as Harper attempted to break Mr. Walter's fall.

Emmett leapt forward, reaching to help the old man to his feet, but Mr. Walter sat dazed on the ground, clutching the handle of his shovel. Harper appeared as if she could spit venom as she regained her footing.

"Why are you fighting?" Harper spit out. "He's on our property."

The Judge boomed. "Those chickens that are destroying my grass aren't on your property. Those sore spots on my green lawn aren't on your property. He is a menace, and you should keep him on a leash. It's time to lock him up in a home."

Harper's green eyes appeared a cloudy gray. "Imagine you of all people making that judgment."

The Judge straightened his slack, unshapely shoulders. "I'm entitled to make whatever judgments I choose, just like I'm entitled to my lawn looking the way I'd like it to look."

Harper crossed her arms across her chest, her eyes trained on him. "I'd suggest that you approach my grandfather like a dignified person fitting your stature. Perhaps be civil for once."

"I've seen your civil, little girl." The Judge sneered. "I wasn't impressed."

"You covered up the murder of my mother and protected her murderer with your connections." Harper leaned forward on the tips of her toes. "I think we all have lines where being civil is thin."

Watching the two of them left Emmett paralyzed. No matter how angry he remained with his grandfather right now, he still had loyalty to him for all he'd done during his childhood, but instinct wanted to protect Harper right now—maybe even from herself. Harper's audacity felt reckless—no one dared challenge this man.

The Judge withdrew from her. "You can't prove that."

Harper shrugged. "It doesn't matter what I can prove. In the court of public opinion, you lost. Maybe show some compassion now and redeem yourself for what you didn't make right back then."

The Judge glared down at Harper. Emmett waited for the reaction. No one spoke to him in this way. The Judge knew someone who owed him a favor that could take care of things for him. Emmett didn't know of anything sinister, but then again he hadn't known about his mother's ordeal either. Right now, he didn't trust his grandfather. This thought made him uneasy.

The Judge jutted his chin out before pivoting and walking back toward the house, shaking his head.

Emmett watched him go, feeling all the tension fleeing his shoulders. Maybe a bit of honesty and confrontation was all it took. The Judge did not avoid these traits within his own home, but he typically didn't embrace them when they were returned.

Glancing back at Harper, he saw her struggling to help Mr. Walter to his feet. Jumping in, he allowed Mr. Walter to put his weight on one shoulder as he lifted himself up.

"The ground feels much further now that I'm old than when I was a young man." His attempt at humor didn't hide his shaking hands and slack jaw.

Harper locked her jaw tight and looked at Emmett with narrowed eyes.

Emmett cleared his throat. "I think we need to get you inside. You may need to rest a bit and recover your energy before you dig again."

Harper nodded. "There's a table of food. We can sneak something out under those old ladies' noses and read Ellis's journal in your office, maybe pick up a few more clues to the hiding spot."

Mr. Walter perked up a bit. "Excellent. I've been wanting a fresh set of eyes on that thing."

Emmett looked out over the lawn as another SUV pulled into the already crowded yard. This one pulled onto the lawn where people didn't usually park, right between the arbor and an old lopsided fountain. As a kid he remembered Harper's mother landscaping the area as one of her weekend projects, but the area had deteriorated with fifteen years of neglect.

Harper's forehead furrowed. "Drats."

Emmett smiled. "An uninvited guest?"

As he said this, Clint stepped out of the driver's seat and a much older couple stepped out of the back seat.

"Clint's parents."

Her puckered lips and furrowed brow left him wondering what was going on in her head. He couldn't quite figure out their relationship, and he found himself wanting to know.

Harper

Putting another dish away into the cabinet, Harper refrained from gritting her teeth together. The constant chatter in the room was grating. If she kept busy, no one expected her to contribute to the conversation, and for all involved, it was best.

Grams had already offered the obligatory invitation for Clint's parent to remain as guests. Harper knew that had been Clint's intentions, and Gloria and Jim didn't know until arrival the invite hadn't been issued beforehand. They'd hemmed and hawed about it, acted put out, but in the end had agreed to stay because Grams had been so gracious, and they really didn't have other plans.

With her eyes, Harper had thrown daggers at Clint every opportunity she had, that is when she wasn't being fawned over or congratulated on finally agreeing to move the wedding up. Clint had neglected to mention that they would not be getting married right now or that he'd been the reason for the delay in a wedding date initially. He'd desired to wait until after he'd become a full-fledged doctor before they'd selected a date.

Now, she appreciated the delay. A divorce would have really

hurt her conservative grandparents; her parents' separation had broken their hearts.

Gloria, Clint's mother, came up behind her and picked up the extra dishtowel.

"I wanted to thank you." She glanced back at Clint and his father who were in a heated discussion about college baseball. "I know it's selfish of me, but I was thrilled when Clint told us that he's decided to take a job at a New Orleans hospital. It's nice that you two will be so close to us instead of states away."

Clint had made many decisions in the thirty-six hours he'd gone in to do a shift at the hospital, and they kept being doled out in small bites for her to absorb and figure out how to react to in front of an audience. She suspected Clint had purposely planned it this way to minimize her reaction.

"He told you this?" Harper kept her voice even, emotionless. She'd had plenty practice keeping the shock from her voice this afternoon.

"Yes." She tilted her head, as if they were keeping secrets. "I know he said it was to be a surprise. Since you've decided to finish your doctorate, he thought this would be his best decision. I was surprised by his sacrifice, and although I should advise him to follow his ambitions, I'm selfish. I hope my only son gives me grandkids at some point, and I'd love for them to be within driving distance."

Harper swallowed against her gut reaction to admit the truth to this woman. She wasn't sure if Clint had convinced himself that all would be forgiven so easily or if he couldn't allow the charade to drop until after the party. Gloria would be crushed.

Gloria winked. "Not that you'll be thinking children right

away, but I spoke to Felipe and he said you aren't working right now. It might be the perfect time."

Harper set down a fine China serving dish. "You spoke to Felipe?"

Gloria set a glass on the counter that she'd dried at least four times over now. "Sure, dear, he calls once a week to check on us. I know he was disappointed that you left him, but he understood."

"I'm sure he did." Harper bristled. Everyone had been living in denial these days. No truth telling going on here, including herself.

Gloria leaned against the counter, the dishtowel hanging in her hands. "Did something happen, Dear?"

Harper turned to look at the two men at the table. "Clint probably should explain what happened." Jim had a brownie lifted to his nose. He sniffed at it, but returned it to the plate, rejecting Grams's offering.

Gloria chuckled. "I know Felipe can be quite ostentatious sometimes. I can't imagine what his poor mother goes through. To think of your son living that lifestyle. I've always been happy that Clint found someone."

Gloria leaned in. "I'll tell you a secret. In high school, I worried that Clint would turn out like Felipe."

Harper's neck jerked towards Gloria, her pulse quickening.

"Don't worry about it, Dear." Gloria smiled. "He's so happy planning his life with you. Makes us so proud."

"Is Clint's sister coming down for the party?" Harper changed the subject quickly before the temptation to reveal the whole sordid tale became too great.

Gloria tsked, her nose contorting in disgust. "She's off gallivanting through a mediation temple. Last month it was rock concerts in Paris. A few months ago she was living in a van in California. A van!"

The woman pulled her shoulders up. "It's such a relief to have one normal child that I don't have to worry about. Clint never disappoints me."

There was loads of pressure in those words. Even Harper felt it, and Gloria with her pristine sweater sets and matching pants wasn't her mother. Clint's eyes were on them, and there wasn't enough distance for him not to have heard.

Emmett

He had it all planned out. The Judge needed a hobby. Preferably something that took time for him to learn and allowed him to meet new people. Although he'd probably insist that his hobby was golf, and even though his short game could use practice, Emmett had nixed that idea. The old man needed to get himself out of his comfort zone, meet new people, and distract himself from Winston's life. Since he'd retired, he'd had his wife and golf. Now, the golf clubs crusted with dust and Grammy had been buried two months ago.

Winston and the Judge could both benefit from a hobby. Of the two men, Emmett figured the Judge would be easier to convince—since both were too stubborn for their own good.

Emmett could pull his grandfather together if he pushed him in the direction of a goal. The old man had always seen life as a task. Even though Emmett's feelings towards his grandfather felt complicated right now because of his mother, he'd promised his grandmother he'd take care of the man, and the obligation weighed heavily on him.

Settled at the dining room table, his grandfather sat smugly, looking over a table laden with dishes. Stepping around the table, Emmett inspected the roasted chicken, the green peas, the glossy mashed potatoes, and a bowl of bread and wondered if a housekeeper had been hired and not just the once every week cleaning lady. It may not be a bad idea. At the least, a housekeeper could provide company for him all day long if he refused to leave the house.

"Come in, Emmett." The Judge motioned widely to the table. "We have a feast today."

Emmett pulled out one of the light oak chairs and took a seat. "What's the special occasion?"

"Can't an old man cook a meal for himself?" He said it with a self-important smirk on his face that spoke of a reason beyond hunger.

"You haven't cooked in twenty years." Emmett pulled bread from the basket, feeling the warmth in his palm. "I still remember that barbeque."

The Judge snorted. "I thought I would turn over a new leaf and handle the neighbor in a different manner. I believe it was the young lady that implied I needed to be more mature."

Emmett regarded the table suspiciously, staring at the bread in his hands and then back to the table. "What did you do?"

The Judge offered a sinister smile in reply. "Eat."

Emmett stared at the table, his mind racing over ideas of poisonings and bodies with holes. Even as he considered the possibilities, he dismissed them as ridiculous. His grandfather wasn't a murderer, a majorly ornery old man, but not a murderer.

Reaching over, the Judge carved himself a leg quarter from

the chicken. "I will eat while it's fresh then. So fresh, you can taste what it ate this morning."

The smug smile on his face was wide, and it dawned on Emmett. "You cooked Mr. Walter's chicken?"

The Judge nodded. "From now on, every time a chicken comes into our yard, we will eat. When he digs a hole, I will plant a rose bush with big thorns. I called your friend for a recommendation. She's going to get back to me with an order."

Emmett shook his head.

The Judge gloated. "I'm doing what you asked."

"This isn't what I asked." Emmett's stomach lurched. Each chicken had a name. Mr. Walter had even painted their names below their nest in the coop. "Have you even considered making amends?"

The Judge's face darkened. "The statue of limitations doesn't run out on murder, Boy. They would take that as a confession."

He inhaled heavily. "Besides, we do what we need to do for our children. Walter understands this."

Emmett doubted that Mr. Walter understood. It was his only daughter that had been taken from him, and although he'd had three sons, it was his daughter who'd always stayed near, a bond Emmett had never felt with any of his own family, but maybe one day he would.

The Judge set his knife and fork down and leaned back in his chair, some of his pride deflated at Emmett's reaction. For Emmett's part, he wished he could release all of the man's pride and get him to feel some empathy.

"How's the job search going?" the Judge asked. "Reconsidered Brooksy's offer?"

Emmett drummed his fingers on the table. "No, I've rented my own place. I'm going solo."

Truthfully, Emmett hadn't figured out if he was going to dabble in antiquities law or the same family law drivel that bored him, but he figured he could figure it out while generating income. Moving in here had felt like a win for him with looking after his grandfather and getting his feet back under him after the closing of the family law firm, but now that he was here, he understood that it should be a temporary arrangement.

The Judge retrieved his fork. "Not an option. Reconsider Brooksy's offer."

Emmett gazed at him, taken aback. Had he just been told no like a child? He was over thirty-years old.

"I wasn't asking permission." Emmett said.

"Don't be obstinate," the Judge said. "I made a deal, and none of us can open up a practice under the family name for five years. Just take a job and be done with it."

Emmett felt a rush in his ears as they burned. "You did what?"

"Hard choices were made," the Judge said. "Consequences for not paying attention to what was going on around you."

Emmett stood up, his chair stubbing against the plush alabaster carpeting. "You didn't even ask if I was okay with this. You agreed to a deal that involved my life and didn't consult me."

"Don't be dramatic," the Judge said, a bite of chicken paused before his lips. "It was necessary."

"No, it wasn't," Emmett said. "You've been so busy trying to protect the screwup that you went and screwed up my life, too."

"Don't overact." The Judge took a bite and then spoke

between mouthfuls. "You can still practice law."

Anger pulsed through Emmett. He felt his plans falling apart around him. "If it means I end up like either of you two, I don't want to."

"Boy, you'd be lucky to be half as good as me or your father in a courtroom," the Judge said, spittle launching across the tablecloth. "You are young and inexperienced and way too arrogant to be either of us."

"I'm just an afterthought." Emmett stood rooted to the carpet as a revelation hit him. "You only see Winston. You will only ever care about what happens to Winston. You only took me from my mother because it was what you thought Winston needed. You didn't care what was best for me. Everything has and will always be about Winston."

"What are you going on about?" The Judge gawked at him. "Of course, I've devoted my life to Winston. He's my only son, my only child."

"Then you two can have each other." Emmett squared his shoulders. "I'm done."

Harper

When she woke up the morning of the party, she had an uneasy quiver in her stomach that, in hindsight, should have been the only sign she needed to call this circus off. But Tara rang the doorbell within minutes of her feet hitting the floor, and the dread quieted. Tara had raided Harper and Clint's apartment with moving boxes and had come with her SUV loaded down with Harper's belongings, which served as an immediate distraction.

Harper had a moment of pity for Clint, feeling guilty about throwing away six years without giving him at least another chance since he was trying so hard. Shouldn't she be able to forgive him? Wasn't that what love that lasted a long time was about? Even as Harper said these words to Tara, she knew she must be experiencing a moment of weakness.

With a sassy snap of her neck, Tara said, "I'm not letting you change your mind and give him another chance. Forget all that forgiveness crap. When someone shows you who they are, believe them."

Harper couldn't disagree with Tara's logic, so while Clint

ushered his parents out to brunch, they carried the boxes inside. As the two laughed and struggled with heavy boxes, the quiver in her middle settled and only offered a twinge every now and then when the engagement party services arrived—tables and chairs, caterer, music, and everyone else Sissy had coordinated.

Grams remained in a constant state of motion, shuttling between her attempts to keep Sissy from permanently rearranging the entire outdoor space to keeping Granddaddy calm and refraining from digging where the party would be in a matter of hours.

In an attempt to be useful, Harper and Tara offered to help the decorator set up, but Sissy shut them down with a few well-chosen remarks about how they were in the way because they had no idea what they were doing.

Since Harper didn't want to continue their argument today when she had enough anxiety about the party, she let the remark slide, even though she did have to keep a lid on Tara, who wasn't quite so discreet with her dislike of the comment. Instead, they spent the afternoon going through Harper's things and preparing for the party—for Tara it was dress and makeup, for Harper, it was building up her mental fortitude.

Come 7:00, they'd finished off a bottle of wine, even though they'd been trying to drink slowly on account of the cases of champagne they'd watched arrive earlier.

Tara pulled a nonexistent piece of lent on the black dress Harper had slipped into—she'd chosen black as if she were in mourning. "Just remember that you can send him back to New Orleans tomorrow morning and go through with the plan. No one has to know what's really going on."

Harper pushed a deep breath through her lips. "Please let everyone be on their best behavior."

Tara had on a skin-tight red number that popped against her copper complexion with its jeweled undertones. Harper wondered if they had invited any single men—right now her mind was blank. "It may be fun if they aren't." Tara smirked, raising her eyebrows. Harper squinted her eyes to imply that it wasn't funny, and Tara threw her hands up. "Kidding. I'll toast to an uneventful night as soon as I have a glass of champagne in hand."

Moments later, they stood outside on an overly decorated patio greeting guests as they spilled in from parking on the front lawn. Light elevator music played over hidden speakers. Sissy had done a phenomenal job, which made Harper suspicious. Harper didn't understand Sissy's motivation for going to all the trouble for this party when she obviously didn't like her cousin. Childhood friendship had dissolved into bitter animosity, even though Harper couldn't say exactly when the line had been crossed.

Uncle Richard approached with a dark amber glass in his hand. "Sissy managed to pull this shindig off, huh? She might be good at something besides complaining."

Harper smiled politely. She wondered how many of those glasses he'd slipped back already. She'd never known Uncle Richard to be a big drinker growing up, but everything else had changed, so why not this, too. Every family seemed to have at least one alcoholic these days.

Harper looked around the people milling around, wondering

where Sissy had disappeared to. "I'm sure she can handle it with her business experience."

He shrugged. "I told her a café was a cute idea but it would fail. So far, she's done okay, but I'll give her a few more years." He grinned as the ice clinked against the glass. "Congratulations on the upcoming marriage. You might want to learn from your mother's mistake, though, and travel with your husband if you want it to work."

Harper frowned. Even though the evening was young, maybe she should get the bartender to cut Uncle Richard off. She'd never seen the good-natured man blunder through a conversation this badly. He'd always been her mother's favorite brother, her favorite uncle. He was losing that distinction quickly.

Tara slid in next to her in a graceful maneuver. "Harper, you need to see this."

Uncle Richard nodded his head and wandered off in the direction of a makeshift bar Sissy had set up off the back porch. Harper scanned the crowd for Sissy or Aunt Effie to warn them, but spotted neither of them among the guests.

She followed Tara past the now repaired fountain and an old arbor—Sissy had certainly been busy today. Tara stopped short and Harper ran into her back. Motioning for Harper to peer around an old evergreen tree that looked newly trimmed, Tara scanned the area for anyone who had followed them.

Standing near the trunk of a large oak tree, Felipe and Clint were standing inches from each other, speaking in hushed tones, a look of intimacy shared between them. As she watched, Felipe reached out and brushed a hand against Clint's arm. Clint didn't move away from him but allowed his hand to remain.

Anger flushed through her, overheating her in the already warm evening air.

Until that moment, she hadn't admitted even to herself that there was a part of her that wanted to believe Clint—that all those years of friendship and his being the one who'd helped her through her father's death hadn't been a waste of years of her life that she couldn't get back. She'd felt sorry for him, for the difficulty of those expectations—from his family, from himself. She'd followed through with this party to help him with those expectations, but he stood here with Felipe, flaunting his defiance of those expectations. She could have saved everyone the trouble. She could have saved herself the embarrassment.

Harper stepped out, ready to pounce.

Tara turned her back to them, crossing her arms across her chest like a bouncer at a nightclub. "I'll keep everyone away."

Harper approached the two, braced for confrontation. With their heads bent towards each other talking furiously in hushed tones, they hadn't noticed her yet.

"You invited the man you cheated on me with to our engagement party?" Harper announced, startling the two. They disengaged and stepped away from each other as if they'd been poked with an electric prod.

"Harper." Felipe smiled weakly, his eyes darting toward Clint. "It's nice to see you. I've missed you. You knew I wanted to make your cake, and I had to insist."

Clint squirmed under Harper's harsh glare.

She shook her head. "What are you doing?"

"Nothing's going on, I swear," Clint said, his expression earnest. "Felipe wanted to be here, to celebrate us."

"How long?" Harper squared her shoulders and braced herself for an answer as she turned toward Felipe. "How long have you two been involved? I want to hear an answer from you."

Felipe swallowed, nervous. Harper never knew the man to be nervous, as he was typically too arrogant to feel concerned. "Harper, Clint wants to be with you. He's told me this himself."

Harper didn't flinch. She knew she needed to hear the truth. "That's not what I asked."

Felipe swallowed. "High school."

Harper glared at Clint. He twisted and withered before her eyes.

"But Harper..." Felipe said.

Harper put her hand up.

Sissy strolled over at that moment, brandishing a bottle of champagne in one hand. Emmett trailed behind her looking uncomfortable, his eyes darting around the scene. Harper could imagine what this looked like.

"Clint and Harper, I need you two to come up to the front to make a toast. Everyone is getting their glasses filled right now."

"The engagement is off." Harper felt the words bounce around them, thudding to the ground.

Tara swooped in, slipping an arm around Harper's middle. "Are you sure you want to do this now?"

"What do you mean the engagement's off?" Sissy asked, the pitch of her voice rising.

Harper turned toward Felipe and Clint, who appeared to crawl under the Mother Mary statue. "Perhaps these two may want to make an announcement, or hell, it's the modern times, it could be their engagement party if Clint would acknowledge who he is."

"Whoa…" Sissy looked from one face to the other, confusion marking her expression.

"I'll take that champagne though." Harper grabbed the bottle and walked off. She waited for relief to come, but it didn't. Only a devastating ache opened up.

"Who's going to announce this?" Sissy called after her.

She hoped the champagne would help the sting fade.

Part III

Emmett

With sunlight pouring directly onto his face from the uncurtained windowsills and the hard planks of flooring jutting into his back, Emmett woke before the sleepy downtown area. He stretched his neck, trying to ease the kinks out of his cramped muscles. If he planned any more campouts in his new office, he'd need an air mattress instead of the salvaged blanket he'd discovered in the trunk of his sedan.

When the party had ended last night, he'd looked over at the darkened, foreboding brick structure of his grandparents' home, one absent his grammy's warmth, and he'd been unable to force himself to walk over. In a hasty decision, he'd followed Jeff and Ellie downtown and decided this was the best place for him to stay.

Now that it was morning, he needed to decide his next steps.

Harper would not be getting married, and in the morning the thought brought a strange energy to his sore, aching muscles.

Sure, the party had been dampened by the whispers—first about why the future bride had deserted the celebration, and then someone had started the rumor that the groom had cheated.

Clint had sat huddled in a corner on the back lawn surrounded by sympathetic friends and family while the Ames family had enjoyed a reunion. And enjoyed they had. The Ames family hadn't skipped a beat and had continued on as if the party had always been meant as a family reunion.

The real kicker was when, after a bottle of champagne, Harper came out and made a toast to Clint and Felipe—the most dysfunctional couple she'd ever encountered.

Tara and Mrs. Patsy had ushered her back inside, while Sissy had smoothed things over by making a joke about champagne and microphones. The party had ended soon after, with many of the uptown guests taking the merriment to the local bars.

Emmett had wanted to attend to Harper but knew that wasn't quite his place. He could give her time to heal and wait for his chance.

After all, he had plenty to attend to in the meantime. One of which was sleeping on the floor in an under-construction office. Hearing footsteps on the stairs behind him, he looked toward the hallway. Moments later, Sissy emerged, hair in a ponytail and circles under her eyes.

She offered him a lopsided smile. "Working on a Sunday?"

He shook his head. "Slept here last night in an attempt to get my head together."

Sissy crossed the room and sank onto the floor across from him. "That feeling's going around this morning."

Emmett ran his fingers through his hair, considering how rumpled he must appear. He'd need to return to his grandfather's house at some point for clothes and a shower. "I'm sure the Ames house is in an uproar."

Sissy twisted a piece of her jean leg, a frown tugging at the corners of her lips. "Clint and his parents were leaving this morning when I loaded the car with the café's serving items. They didn't even speak to me. Clint looked miserable."

Emmett's chest lurched. "What about Harper?"

Sissy shook her head, raising her perfectly groomed eyebrows. "She hasn't come out of her room. Grams claims Harper's not upset, but she's angry that Clint made her go through with the party. Something about a second chance."

Emmett nodded, chewing over this in his head. He'd known something was going on, though he couldn't have guessed it was something like this.

"You want a second chance, right?" Sissy said, stretching her legs out. She glanced at him and then looked away. "With Harper, I mean."

Emmett studied her, noticing the nervous twitch to her lips.

She exhaled, and it bounced around the empty room. "I never really had a chance, huh?"

Emmett saw her desire reflected in her hazel eyes.

He tapped her leg. "Sissy, you and I have always been friends. Most of the time growing up I wasn't sure if you even liked me at all as even a friend, but I've always considered you one of my closest friends, even back then."

Sissy's eyes watered, and she kept her gaze on her shoes. "I always knew you wouldn't notice me with Harper around. I thought— well, I believed—when she left, you might finally realize that I was here, too. But you only noticed that I was an Ames and kept me around because you wanted to be near my family."

"Come on, Sissy," Emmett said, bumping her foot with his. He felt awful. He'd suspected there was something going on with Sissy, and he should have handled it differently. "I always thought of the three of us as this team. I'll admit to loving your family, but it feels like nothing has been right in my life since the three of us were playing explorers in the backyard."

Sissy smiled, her eyes watery with unshed tears. "We all grew up since then. No more being bossed around by you two."

"You know you liked it." Relieved to have her smiling, he hoped to steer her away from the serious territory.

"I did not," she proclaimed in mock indignation. "I liked being part of the group though. Always my downfall."

"Not a downfall." Emmett bumped against her leg again, trying to coax her into the easy camaraderie he knew she was capable of. "We were part of something special."

Sissy gazed at him a moment, considering, weighing his words against her memories. He knew her so well he could see it happening behind her eyes. Then she nodded.

"You should work things out with Harper." Emmett leaned back on his elbow, trying to ease the tightness in his lower back. "You two would be better as a team."

She bit down on her bottom lip. "She'll never understand what I've done."

"Try her." Emmett knew she couldn't have done anything that bad. Sissy had always been prim and proper, an example of moral fortitude.

"Her mother's ring is gone," Sissy croaked out. "I can't get it back."

Emmett swallowed against the harsh swear that rose in him.

He'd hoped that the whole ring situation had been a misunderstanding.

Every time he thought he was getting closer to joining the three back as a team, he took another step back.

Harper

The brownie container felt warm to her touch. Grams must have taken them out the oven right before she'd knocked on Harper's door to persuade her to come downstairs for her special recipe. When Harper hadn't responded to her pleas, she'd said she'd leave them out on the kitchen counter just for her. Emerging from her room after everyone had settled in for the night, Harper felt the warmth of the kitchen, remnants of Grams's oven working overtime.

Harper could raid the refrigerator for leftover dinner, but the brownies appealed more to her after a day of a champagne headache, queasy stomach, and memories of embarrassing herself last night.

On first bite, tiny rays of warmth spread through her. Maybe last night hadn't gone as badly as she believed. If chocolate brownies still existed in the world, things couldn't be that awful.

Strolling in from the living area, Sissy's critical eyes zoned in on the container of brownies in front of Harper and narrowed. Harper had believed she was alone, especially since Sissy had her own house to be residing in at this time of the night.

Sissy pulled out the chair and slid in across the table from her. "If you're done feeling sorry for yourself, I need to talk to you."

"You really need to work on your empathy. Humans show that for each other, you know?"

Sissy furrowed her brows in a thin line. "I'm not good at it, I know. Add it to the ever growing list of complaints."

"Here, I'll show you how it's done." Harper scooped a brownie out of the pan and pushed it towards her. "What's bothering you?"

Sissy's lips thinned further as a wrinkle formed in the middle of her forehead. A moment passed between them where they measured each other up. Harper thought about the little girls they'd been, both bossy and independent, daring each other to be better than they were. Was this how the two girls grew up? Two competitive women who pettily argued with each other instead of motivating and inspiring the other to be better.

She preferred the dynamics between the two young girls.

"I sold your mother's ring," Sissy said. "And I can't get it back."

Harper took a bite of brownie and chewed. She told herself that she'd known this, but hearing her confess it aloud felt different. Final. It was really gone.

She swallowed against the chocolate that had thickened in her mouth. "Why?"

Sissy swallowed, her fingers fiddling with the brownie.

"When I wanted to open the café, I needed capital."

"So you sold my mother's ring?" The words spilled out. Harper immediately regretted them. She'd decided to be more like the girl she'd been, and she wasn't off to a good start.

Sissy sighed and then nibbled on the brownie. "I don't suppose these things have bourbon or something stronger in them?"

"Who knows what Grams's secret ingredients are," Harper said. "But I think I had enough alcohol last night."

"I didn't sell it, per se." Sissy said, looking into Harper's eyes. "It's a complicated story."

Harper squirmed in her chair, getting comfortable. "Let's hear it then."

Sissy nodded. "First, I went to my dad for a loan because I couldn't get one from the bank. My father had paid for everything I owned until that point, so I had no credit."

Harper continued chewing on her brownie. Uncle Richard had always given Sissy everything—cars, apartments, college, and her credit card bill paid every month.

Sissy frowned as she broke off a piece of brownie. "He wouldn't loan me the money. He said restaurants were bad investments and that I would get bored as soon as it became difficult."

Harper frowned. Uncle Richard hadn't been so harsh growing up. In fact, he'd spoiled Sissy. Last night at the party, he hadn't been particularly nice either. What had turned the man bitter in the years Harper had been away? No one had spoken about this change.

"I couldn't give up my dream, but I didn't have that kind of cash." Sissy popped the brownie in her mouth and sank back into her chair.

Harper could tell she was contemplating how she told the next part. She recognized the familiar defenses and calculations within her green eyes.

Finally, she straightened her spine but continued staring down at the brownie. "I was seeing Hunter Wells at the time."

"Wells?" Harper ran through everyone she knew from the area, recalling a familiarity with the name. "As in the Wells family?"

Sissy nodded.

The family dabbled in a little of everything. A few chain restaurants, a few offshore boats, real estate, and who knows what else. Slightly older, Hunter Wells had been a few years ahead of Harper in school so she didn't know him, but everyone spoke about the family. Mixed reviews on that end.

"He and I made a deal," Sissy said bitterly. "He loaned me fifteen thousand with the ring as collateral. I would pay him back over the first five years of the business. I didn't see how anything could go wrong."

She tapped on the table, anger sketching lines into her forehead. "Six months later, a blonde drops in at the shop wearing the ring."

Harper inhaled sharply. She knew the sting of that betrayal. The rawness hadn't dulled yet.

Sissy offered a crooked smile with piercing eyes. "An engagement announcement appeared in the paper a few weeks ago. Mom called me."

Harper could see the pain had not dulled for Sissy. She hoped this would not be her two years from now still bitter over Clint's betrayal. "You have Emmett, though."

Sissy laughed, a harsh empty sound. "He and I aren't a couple. He's still hung up on you after all these years."

Harper leaned back in her chair. "They why?" She couldn't

even finish the thought. Her mind raced with confusion.

Sissy shrugged. "I wanted him to be interested in me. I didn't want to feel like a failure, to feel like I was alone. As my father always reminds me every chance he gets, your life was such a success in comparison. Emmett's such a good friend and didn't want to hurt my feelings, but he can't pretend feelings that aren't there."

Harper swiped at a chocolate crumb with her finger. "I wouldn't compare your life to mine. My fiancé cheated on me with his best friend, who happens to be my boss. So I lost my job and my fiancé all in one moment that I wish I could erase from my visual memories, mind you. Not much success there."

Sissy's eyebrows rose. "We Ames women aren't doing so well in the love department, but that job wasn't you anyway. I remember those Easy Bake oven cakes you made. Terrible."

Harper laughed. She hadn't thought of those cakes they'd made in a long time. "Does anything taste good from that plastic oven?"

Sissy's eyes sparkled with laughter. "Hey, I made the best cookies."

They looked at each other. A moment of understanding passing between them. Maybe a truce was possible. If they could learn to let things go.

"You should give Emmett a chance." Sissy crossed her arms over her chest. "He's the best man either you or I will ever know."

Harper plucked up another brownie. "Sissy, I can't erase the past, but I can't keep living there either. It hurts too much."

Emmett

In the Bittersweet Café, charming couples occupied all the window tables, but he could use this to his advantage. Choosing a bistro table in the back corner where he could isolate himself and his mother from the engrossed faces bent over the strawberry French toast special, he hoped to avoid a scene with whatever she'd hoped to talk to him about today.

Keeping his eyes on the door, he tapped on the paper napkin holder to settle his nerves. Why he'd agreed to meet Toni, his mother, for brunch, he couldn't say. Sleeping in a rented out commercial space had left him antsy and ready to take action— but he didn't know what action yet.

Toni swooped inside, her eyes sweeping the area before falling onto him in the corner of Sissy's café.

He squirmed. After everything he'd learned, he felt uncomfortable facing her. He probably should apologize, but his desire to do so was conflicted. The Hebert men had treated her poorly, but a nagging voice kept at him, telling him that she could have told him the truth at any time. Everything had been a lie, and she'd been part of the deceit. He couldn't get a handle on how he felt about that just yet.

She slipped into the seat, eyes on him. "I'm thrilled you agreed to meet me."

He wished she would look around the café so that he could take a moment to breathe and figure out where the shield of animosity he protected himself against her attempts at kindness had gone.

He swallowed instead. "I was surprised you called."

Her calls had grown more infrequent through the years, but to be fair, he hadn't given the woman much to hang onto growing up.

She frowned, studying him, her eyes lingering too long over his, making him uncomfortable. "Your dad called me."

Emmett picked up the red coffee mug. This wasn't the way to start a conversation and make him feel more at ease. Winston never had anything good to say concerning Emmett.

She raised her eyebrows. "He says you're not going home, that you and your grandfather have had a falling out."

Setting the mug down, he considered Winston's motives. Usually selfish in nature, there had to be something. "We aren't seeing eye to eye on things right now. I overestimated my ability to take care of the stubborn man."

She stretched her delicate hands across the table, allowing them to rest in the middle. "I know about the deal with the law firm and not being able to use your name." She tilted her head and her brown eyes softened. "It's not as bad as it seems right now."

He leaned back and folded his arms across his chest, some of the old anger returning. "I'm not willing to let someone else pull the strings of my life. I didn't agree to this sacrifice." They'd all allowed the old Judge to dish out the final verdicts as if they were in his courtroom and his judgment couldn't be questioned. Although fine in the courtroom, families weren't supposed to work this way. Growing up, he'd learned how a family should be from watching the Ames family; otherwise, he may have believed this dysfunction was normal.

"I know, Son." She twiddled her fingers on the table. He noticed that her wedding ring was absent. In fact, he couldn't remember her ring finger being encumbered by jewelry the last two times he'd seen her. "Your dad and I have an idea about how to fix this."

He studied her, wondering about the amount of time Winston spent talking to his mother, but this concocted idea would need to take precedence over his concern about his parents rekindling a toxic romance.

She rushed ahead. "You may not like it, and you may consider it worse than the alternative of not being able to start your own practice."

"What?" Emmett asked, feeling irritated that the two had cooked up some idea—even more irritated that they'd been planning his life together. "Are you suggesting I be adopted by another family? Because I thought of that numerous times growing up with neither a father nor mother around."

A frown twisted at her lips, and her shoulders jerked upwards with her deep breath, but she shook it off. "Take my last name. Your dad thoroughly checked the papers your grandfather signed, and he believes it is a loophole."

Emmett leaned back in the chair, trying to absorb this idea.

His mother's last name. Rodrigue. It was an odd thought—like divorcing his family. Did he want to take that final of a step? Perhaps. His own father suggesting it made it even more ironic since he would be the last to carry the family name as the only son of an only son.

Did Winston have an ulterior motive? Emmett's suspicions worked overtime. "You and Winston worked this out?" Winston helping him didn't feel right. Had it taken thirty years for his parents to work out co-parenting? He wasn't buying it.

She fiddled with her fingers on top of the table. With a clean face, hair down, and jeans, she looked no more than a few years older than him. A decade at the most.

"It was your father's idea. I agree that it is a good one."

Even if Winston had a different motive, Emmett couldn't deny that this would solve his conundrum. His plans for the future could continue without him having to create new plans.

A bell jangled, causing Emmett to automatically look toward the door. Winston strolled through, clutching rolled up papers in his right hand. In jeans and a green polo shirt, he didn't look out of place for the café crowd, but with a clean-cut appearance, the man who'd been on a binge for two weeks looked unrecognizable.

His twitchy eyes and revolving grip on the papers gave the impression that he hadn't spent more than five minutes recovering before stepping outside though.

He yanked a free chair from a nearby table and sank onto it. Grabbing Emmett's coffee mug from the black napkin, he released the papers onto the table and lifted the mug to his mouth with a shaky grip.

Emmett watched as his mother retrieved the papers, but she also placed one hand on Winston's unsteady arm. Setting the mug down, Winston inhaled deeply.

Winston shrugged, his eyes bloodshot with black circles underneath. "I drew up the papers and called in a favor. If you agree to it, it will be a done deal."

Emmett regarded the papers suspiciously. His family appeared to have a way of doing things, not necessarily the legal or moral way.

Emmett took the papers from his mother's outstretched hand. "Why do you want me to do this?"

"Kid." Winston pushed the mug away, the left side of his mouth curving into a smirk. "I figure we didn't really do much right by you. Maybe doing it on your own will give you a better shot at beating this family's curse."

Emmett didn't know how he could disagree with Winston on that one.

Harper

She peeked into the office and didn't see her granddaddy's silvery hair bent over his desk. She scanned the room, her eyes lingering a moment over the dusty battle models and the growing stack of newspapers near the recliner. He used to toss those out every Sunday, but from the number of folds, it looked like at least three months worth now.

"Granddaddy?" She felt foolish speaking to an empty room, but Grams had said he'd come in here to read before lunch.

"Have you seen the mill?" Granddaddy asked, his voice muffled, coming from behind the desk area.

Harper walked around a stack of old trunks that held postcards from the 1930s. He'd painstakingly wrapped his parents' postcards in plastic to preserve them. When she'd been fourteen, she'd read through them and concluded that her great grandfather was quite the romantic. She'd also concluded that she'd been born into the wrong generation if she expected any of the boys she'd known to be that romantic—including Emmett, who by that time, she'd considered her boyfriend. She didn't know anyone who would call her love, bring her flowers, and speak in proclamations of undying love.

Spread out on the floor behind the desk and overstuffed leather chair, Granddaddy had a scaled drawing of the property, some old writings, Ellis's journal, and a history book on the war spread before him. A chick of hair flipped over into his eyes and another piece flipped toward the opposite side of his part, nearly straight up, making him look dishelved. His reading glasses sat on the bridge of his nose, and the look on his face gave away that he was worked up.

"It's time for lunch, Granddaddy." Harper kneeled down, trying to soften her towering stance.

He ran his fingers over the drawing. "I can't find the mill. The old well is still there, covered though. The old tractor barn is right here." He jabbed at a splotch on the drawing. "There were three servants' houses and an outdoor kitchen. All gone. A few bricks from the chimney to mark their spot."

Harper frowned. She hated seeing him like this. "Why don't you think about it while we eat? Food always makes the brain work better."

His forehead creased. "The main house lay one hundred feet from the kitchen, and the mill was seventy-five feet from the kitchen. But it's not there."

Sissy strolled into the room. "The woman says if her fried chicken gets cold, we will be fried."

"Granddaddy." Harper felt the anxiety coming off of him as if it were an electrical current. "I'm sure it's there. Let's go get some of Grams's chicken, and then I will help you think it through. If Grams fries us in her grease, neither of us is going to find the mill."

Sissy walked around the desk and the two exchanged looks.

"A chicken's missing." Granddaddy put his hands on the drawing, rubbing his fingers along the light lines scribbled onto the diagram. "Betsy, I called her. She had these six red feathers and liked to wander. I can't eat Betsy."

"Patsy didn't cook Betsy," Sissy said. "She would never kill a chicken herself."

"Chicken coop." Granddaddy ran his finger over a line on the drawing that appeared to be where the structure should be. Harper could see overlapping structures, but she couldn't read the labels from her upside down position.

"Granddaddy," Harper said, putting her hand on his arm. "You love Grams's cooking. You can bring your drawing for us to look at while we eat."

"The mill," Granddaddy said.

Grams entered the room; her eyes sweeping over the three of them huddled in back of the small space between the desk and the wall with Granddaddy still on the floor.

She steadied herself with a hand on the back of the recliner. "Walter, my food is getting cold, and you know I don't like to serve you cold food. Let's go to lunch and then figure this all out later."

His eyes fell on her and his heavy breathing calmed some.

He nodded, and Sissy and Harper moved in to help him to his feet. Once he'd regained his balance, Harper swiped at the items on the floor so he wouldn't trip over them as he followed Grams out of the room. The two walked hand in hand, Grams holding him close.

Sissy waited for them to be gone before she turned to Harper and shook her head. "Sometimes I think the treasure gives him something to hold on to. But then, sometimes I wonder if it's healthy for him to cling so tightly. You know what I mean?"

Harper nodded. "I just don't see how it could be found. It's such a long shot."

"Oh, I don't know," Sissy said, putting a hand on her hip. "If anyone could figure it out, I'm sure it's him. You too, of course. You two were always so much alike."

Harper studied the letters clutched in her hand. History typically held the answers to life's mysteries, at least that's what she'd learned in all her years of schooling.

Perhaps she could figure out where the family heirlooms were buried from the work her granddaddy had already done.

Emmett

Emmett gripped the building lease papers tightly in his hand. He'd wanted to be the one to deliver the news to his grandfather, and it had gone as well as he'd expected. The old man had fumed, threatened to cut him out of the will – an empty threat since Grammy had designated his inheritance upon her death. Besides, it didn't matter. For the chance to start over, he'd risk being penniless. He'd simply told his grandfather all these things and watched the old man grow quiet and refuse to speak.

Now that he'd delivered the news, he wanted to keep things rolling, so with lease papers in hand, he headed next door to turn them over. Coming around the row of live oaks and camellia bushes, he nearly tripped over a fallen tree branch as he took in the scene before him.

He stood still a moment, watching Harper pull a tape measure across the yard, while Sissy gripped a large paper drawing, which he thought might be blue prints in her hand. Orange flags littered the grass. As he studied the odd scene before him long enough, he realized that the flags appeared to be forming shapes of some kind, not just some haphazard scattering.

"Twenty-five, right?" Harper called out, shading her eyes with the hand gripping an orange flag.

Sissy turned the drawing in different directions, puzzling over it. "Yes, but the other wall is twenty-seven. I don't think these people built with rulers."

Harper stuck an orange flag into the ground, and Emmett finished his walk over, curious as to what these two were doing. Even the fact that they were working together had him stumped.

Sissy smiled as he approached, the pinkness of her forehead and bare shoulders revealing they'd been at whatever this was for a while.

"I came to deliver the signed lease papers," he said, waving the papers for Sissy to see. "But now I have to know what is going on here."

He watched as Harper began stepping out a new measurement. Now that he stood close, he could see that the flags had string attached to them, creating makeshift walls. Taking giant steps in Mr. Walter's oversized rubber boots, she rolled out the string to the next marker. With her hair in a ponytail and her white T-shirt and shorts, she looked just like the fifteen-year-old girl who'd held his heart.

"Treasure hunting." Sissy grinned. "Did you get everything worked out with your grandfather?"

"Somewhat." He frowned, looking down at the large rolled out paper in Sissy's hands. The entire situation still made him uneasy, but he'd decided to keep moving forward. "I have a new last name—Rodrigue. Talk about plenty of paperwork, but I'm going to look at it as a fresh start."

"Your mama's name, huh?" Sissy said, squinting against the

sun to peer closely at him. "Not something you hear everyday."

Emmett gestured toward the grid. "This isn't something you see everyday either."

Sissy laughed. "That's all Harper. Although she's claiming I inspired her."

Emmett watched as Harper sunk a flag into the ground. "How exactly are you treasure hunting?"

Sissy shrugged. "She says we need to see it. She's marking out all the old structures that no longer exist but that existed in 1863."

"Do you know what structure the treasure was buried near?"

Harper glanced back at them and called out. "Next measurement."

Sissy glanced down at the drawing. "Twenty-six and a half."

Harper placed her hand on her hip and scanned the ground around her. "Are you sure?"

Sissy tried putting her finger on the structure without removing her hand that was holding the document, but her fingers didn't reach. Emmett moved in and took ahold of the side of the sketch. Sissy glanced up at him, but she looked back down and her finger found the pencil marks that had been painstakingly written next to the far right side.

"Yes," Sissy called out. "I told you they didn't measure anything."

Emmett watched as Harper shrugged and then put the tape measure against the flag and began to walk it out.

Sissy sighed. "She hasn't figured out what structure yet, but she's decided to find out. She's chosen to write her dissertation on the Ames folklore and others like it. Apparently, we are not the only family who buried our valuables in the backyard during the Civil War. I hope the others at least used a map."

Emmett nodded. "And you're helping?"

She grinned. "What else do I have to do on my day off?" Emmett noticed that the constant stress scowl she typically wore had disappeared. He wondered what had happened between the two. He was happy for whatever it was though. It meant they were one step closer to being that team he'd imagined.

"I'm going to help," he said, taking off his jacket. "It will be like those adventures we had as kids."

"Oh, Emmett," Sissy said, her eyebrows rising in sympathy. "I don't know if Harper is ever going to want to go back to the those times, the past I mean. I think it's difficult for her."

"Remember," he said, squeezing her arm. "I'm no longer an Hebert. It's like she's meeting a whole new person."

He strolled out to help with the measuring and placing of orange flags, feeling excitement creeping into his oxfords.

Harper

Harper stretched her toes out and they brushed against the discarded plates and glasses on the coffee table. Somewhere in the house a clock ticked the early morning hour, but she couldn't sleep like the two passed out: one on the armchair, and the other on the sofa. Sissy had drifted to sleep first, having only stayed for moral support. Emmett had lasted longer, having drifted to sleep as she'd begun rereading Ellis's journal.

It was like one of those logic puzzles her eighth grade teacher would put on the board every morning, except her teacher gave them the answer at the end of the day. No one had the answer to tell her if she was on the right track or veering off course. It didn't make the puzzle any less intriguing.

Ambrose had written three letters home. In the first one, he'd mentioned nothing about the family heirlooms—only written to reassure his mother that he was all right, and he hoped she wouldn't be too angry with him. In the second letter he'd spoken about coming home to help make cane syrup. A seemingly innocent comment. In the third letter, he said "Ellis, remember sitting out back chewing on the sugar cane stalks? Remember me when you are napping out back."

All of this could be a boy homesick as he fought in a brutal war that took his life after only months of leaving home. But in his effects returned to his mama by a fellow local soldier was the one letter his mama had written to him that had made it his way. She'd told him that Ellis did not remember where the heirlooms had been buried. Her letter was dated after his first one.

Knowing that the letters could have been read by anyone along the way to its home, had Ambrose chosen to include a cryptic message? Granddaddy believed so. If this premise was true, then they had a general location. She'd need to comb through the journal, though, to look for any hints as to where the two brothers would have napped.

Granddaddy had been rambling about the mill, and Harper was convinced he was right. The mill had to be it, but the exact dimensions of the old mill wasn't certain either, as it had never appeared on any land surveys. It had been a makeshift structure for personal stock. Its rusted tin and recycled wood not lasting long in terms of the long history of Ames family on the property.

Grams's slippers snapped against the floor. "Are you still awake?"

Harper lowered Ellis's journal. "Can't sleep with this on my mind."

Grams bent over and picked up the plates. "You aren't going to solve it in one day. Your granddaddy has been working on it since he retired."

Harper chewed on her bottom lip, mulling over all she'd learned. Granddaddy had gathered together much information. If his health would have been better, Harper had no doubt he would have figured it out by now. She had no doubt that his memory lapses had prevented him putting the details together.

"I'm going to clean this up, Grams," Harper said. "Get some sleep."

Grams sank down onto a chair. "I'm happy to see the three of you together again. Makes my heart happy."

Harper traced the edge of the journal with her finger. "Nothing's the same though. Everything feels complicated."

Grams tilted her silk-wrapped head to the side. "Oh, honey, we can't stop the world from changing, but there's a specialness here that you can hang onto even as life shifts from under you."

"I'm sorry about the party." Harper leaned her head back against the sofa, feeling heavy. "I should have told you the truth from the beginning."

Grams waved her hand in the air. "No worries here. The family had a great time, and it was a good night for your granddaddy. I can't ask for more. I'm sorry the engagement won't work out, even though I never quite thought you two were right for each other."

Harper studied Grams a moment, chewing on her bottom lip as she considered the older woman's strength. She'd been married to Granddaddy since she was nineteen, and she still loved him. Harper could only hope for that one day.

"I don't know what I'm going to do with my life yet. I think I'm going to run the store."

Grams smiled, standing. "Don't rush it, Honey. If that's what you want to do, then you can have it, but don't you feel like you have to do it. I don't ever want to be a burden, not to you or to Sissy."

Harper nodded, feeling the smooth leather of the journal with her thumb. "I just remember when I was a little girl, I knew. You know what I mean? I knew I was going to be just like Granddaddy when I grew up. I don't know when everything became so confusing."

Grams leaned on the back of the chair for support. "Your mother's death made us all question what was right, but I do know that she would want you to remember who you are. Your roots, I mean. Remember how she fixed things with her hands, restored all those antique houses. Even though all three brothers went to college and got fancy jobs, she stayed true to herself and did what made her happy. She'd want that for you, too."

Harper nodded. For so long she'd only felt anger and grief over her mother's death, and it had clouded all areas of her life. Perhaps she simply needed to remember who she was before that dark cloud had settled on top of her.

Grams leaned down to plant a kiss on her forehead. "Get some rest, Honey. Your granddaddy will be ready to dig tomorrow."

Harper smiled. With the flags, her granddaddy's plans for digging had become more focused. He'd spent time sketching them out today. With the journal, Harper hoped to pinpoint exactly where they needed to dig. Her granddaddy had gone off to bed promising to have all his energy built up for a dig tomorrow, and she wanted it to be a carefully selected spot.

The answer to where to dig was in this journal. It had to be.

Emmett

He woke with a start. Harper hovered inches from his face, a sweet smell of flowers surrounding her. Outside the windows, it must still be nighttime. He sat up, scanning the room, and his eyes fell on Sissy, asleep on the sofa.

Harper whispered. "I need your help."

She stepped back, and he noticed she was clutching the journal and a sheet of paper against her chest.

He struggled to his feet, feeling the adrenaline pumping from the sudden waking. He must have drifted off to sleep while waiting for Harper to read and talk it over with them. The last he remembered was young Ellis's harrowing encounter with his mama when she discovered he didn't remember where they'd buried the trunk. The nine year old had quite the story-telling ability or a knack for exaggeration. It was difficult to tell which having never met the man—young or old.

He stretched, his back tight from the sitting position. "What time is it?"

"Three thirty."

"In the morning?" he admonished, following her toward the

doorway. "Should we wake Sissy?"

Harper glanced back, a smile on her face, a laugh at him still sparkling in her eyes. "She has work in the morning. Do you think it's a good idea?"

Sissy groaned. "I'm awake. If you wanted to let me sleep, you should really learn to be quieter."

Harper laughed. "I tried."

Harper's spirits were high. Emmett had the feeling that she'd had some kind of breakthrough in the mystery of the missing heirlooms, and his own excitement began to grow.

Sissy stood and stretched. "This better be good."

Harper led them toward the back of the house. "Follow me to find out."

Outside, the humidity wrapped its arms around them, swelling their lungs. The sun had beat down all day, and the darkness had provided little relief.

Harper led them toward the chicken yard and beyond where the fruit tree orchid now stood. Pulling out a flashlight she had buried somewhere in the depths of the items snuggled tightly to her chest, she shined it around the grass.

Emmett followed the beam of the flashlight as it moved from the orange flag to a line right beyond the citrus trees. "What are we looking for?"

Harper strolled over to the tree line. "Nothing says exactly where the old mill was located."

Sissy stopped walking and crossed her arms over her chest.

"But Ellis wrote that the wood shed was next door to the mill, which made the work of getting the fire started under the cauldron easier."

Emmett glanced back at the orange flags they'd laid out earlier marking the old woodshed. The dimensions roughly matched the chicken coop minus the fence on the other side.

Sissy stepped sideways to overlook the scene. "How do we know it's the mill again?"

Emmett walked toward the flags. Runoff from the roof had created a dip in the ground here. Maybe the two structures had shared runoff at one time since the ditch that had been whittled into the ground was deep. With the threat of fire at a mill, though, that seemed an unlikely scenario. Florian Ames more than likely would have left some distance to protect the firewood.

Harper set the journal and her notes down, keeping her grip on the flashlight. "Ambrose tried to tell them in his letters, but Ellis completely missed the hints. However, in his journal he wrote about the times spent with his brother. He missed him."

"So Ellis never figured out it was the mill?"

Harper crouched down, feeling around the grass. "No, he thought they were near the tractor barn. It was a case of him being certain of an idea and not seeing the evidence to prove him wrong."

"But the mill still leaves plenty area to dig," Sissy added, her tone having a hint of a whine to it.

Emmett remembered their few middle of the night escapades and how cranky Sissy could get. Perhaps this was why Harper had tried to leave her asleep.

"Not necessarily," Harper said, "Ambrose said that they sat out back chewing sugar cane stalks and napping."

Emmett moved in closer to see what she was groping on the ground for. "Does that give you a location?"

"Ellis said in his journal that his Paw planted squash along the back wall except for where they kept the oyster shells. I'm figuring they didn't sleep in the squash."

"Wait just one minute." Sissy pounded her foot on the ground for emphasis. "How could he forget where he's at if they were in the middle of an oyster bed?"

Harper laughed. "Glad you're awake. Apparently, our great, great, oh however many greats Grand-père Florian put them everywhere around each building for drainage run off. Drove his wife crazy because she preferred rose bushes."

Emmett hunched down beside her and began pushing around in the grass as she was. Sissy walked back toward the house, but neither of them called her back. Sissy would always be Sissy.

He'd dropped to his knees and was feeling around in a low spot when Sissy returned with a shovel in hand. "You two are hopeless."

She handed the shovel over to him, and he instinctively dug into the low spot. Beneath the initial layer of dirt, his shovel scraped against another material, sounding like metal scratching a chalkboard. Harper stood and walked over, eyes fastened to the grey tool, waiting for him to unearth its objects.

Emmett pulled up on the shovel and dumped its contents over. Under the beam of the flashlight a few chips of oyster shells peppered the chunk of dirt. Shining the flashlight into the hole, all their heads bent over to see layers of oyster shells below.

Harper

Staring down into the abyss of dirt and oyster shells, the possibility that she was wrong nagged at the coattails of her thoughts, but she couldn't see how. She'd moved the pieces around of this puzzle in every possible scenario she could imagine. She'd written the clues down, drawn arrows, erased, starred – everything to figure it out on paper and in her head. It's not as if her ancestors had tried to trick them with misleading clues. They'd simply not spelled it out so that no one else could steal the family's wealth.

"What do we do?" Emmett asked, shovel paused in his hand, looking to her for answers.

Harper's stomach flip-flopped. She'd been so certain when she sat in the room in her own thoughts, now she hoped she didn't disappoint anyone. "We need to get Walter."

"Are you crazy?" Sissy asked. "It's four o'clock in the morning."

Harper met Sissy's wide eyes. "Do you think he'd care about the time if we told him we found it without him?"

Sissy nodded, giving a crooked grin. "Good point."

Harper shifted the light around, trying to see more, trying to see if she was right. "Do you want to go get him or me?"

Sissy laughed. "I'll get him. Your excitement might kill him."

Sissy walked away from the group, but Harper noticed a slight spring in her step. The woman may take awhile to warm up, but she could be fun when the occasion called for it.

Emmett shoved the shovel deep into the ground. "Do you feel that?"

Harper looked to him, puzzled. His smile deepened.

He leaned on the shovel. "The air. It's telling us this is right."

She offered him a crooked smile. "You haven't changed since you were twelve, you big doof."

"That's reassuring," Emmett said, chuckling. "You liked me back then."

"I tolerated you," she said, softening it with a smile. "Sissy was the easy one."

She would not admit that she still liked him in the present. The darkness and the electric air made everything confusing.

He chuckled. "I see you and Sissy's truce has made you see the past with a blurred lens. I guess you forgave her for the ring then?"

Harper shrugged. Of all people, Harper knew what it felt like for the person you loved to betray you. She could not hold the ring against Sissy when she'd lied to Grams and Granddaddy and embarrassed them and herself. They'd both learned bitter lessons about love, and hopefully they'd make better choices in the future. But since they were stubborn, they'd probably repeat the mistake a few times.

"Maybe it's time to leave the past where it belongs, and move onto a guilt free future."

Emmett lifted the shovel. "Says the person about to dig up history."

His grin radiated charm even under the wonky shadows being cast by the light of the moon streaming through the fruit trees. His mussed hair only added to the boyishness of his appeal. He'd missed his calling by becoming a lawyer. He'd always been meant for adventure and the outdoors—something the Heberts didn't know much about.

"The past is confusing," she said, blowing her hair out of her face. "Digging up these family heirlooms allows me to feel hope about Granddaddy. Maybe his mind can rest a little easier, you know?"

Emmett nodded and dug the shovel into the oyster hole and turned it out. He dug quietly, his shirt rippling under the pressure. He seemed to enjoy the task, but Harper felt listless just watching him. Why hadn't he grown bald or paunchy? Her heart would have a much easier time closing itself to him. It sounded superficial even in her head, but she desperately searched for some reason to not put her heart through the torture.

A bright light bounced up and down in their direction, and Sissy and Granddaddy came into view as they cleared the last tree.

"I hear we have treasure to dig," Granddaddy said, his voice alert and robust. He was walking faster than she'd seen his pace in awhile.

Harper laughed, feeling the excitement rush back through her. "I know it's here, Granddaddy. Just you wait."

He grinned, his face beaming under the luminescent lighting. "I knew you'd find it."

"Hurrah," Sissy muttered. "We haven't found anything yet."

Emmett called from the mounting pile of dirt and oyster shells. "I think I have something."

Tearing into the earth, Emmett had focused in on a four-foot by five-foot area that held a layer of oyster shells. He'd dug three feet deep in one area and the dark edge of something solid noticeably stuck out of the dirt.

He gently passed the shovel around the object, while Harper dropped down to her belly and ran her fingers along the edge. The mud formed a slimy layer around the slats. As Emmett scrapped away at the shells and dirt stuck to the surface, a rusted metal strip wrapped around the edge revealed itself. An old steamer trunk, not an incredibly large one, began to take form.

Grabbing an oyster shell, Harper used it as a makeshift tool to help with the scraping away of the debris, as Emmett further loosened the packed layers from all sides.

Granddaddy stood above, holding the lantern so that it cast a glow over the entire scene.

"You call that a flat-top trunk or steamer trunk. These were designed for steamboats and trains. That it's small helps dates it. The smaller packers were practical for ships." He coughed, a great hacking sound brought on by the dampness and heat. The light bounced around. Sissy stepped close to him and steadied his arm. "Probably brought over when Great Grand-mère traveled from France."

According to the journal, the boy had found it in the attic. Ambrose had thought it was thick enough to protect the valuables from the elements. Ellis had hoped they wouldn't get a switch if the trunk were indeed valuable itself. He'd been cross with his brother. It was no fair being the youngest and being bossed around and not listened to when he spoke.

Perhaps since it had taken over a century to locate this nefarious box, Ambrose should have listened to his brother's childish antics, as the child soldier had put it. But then again, the four of them wouldn't be here tonight, feeling the excitement crawl inside and outside their flesh.

Reaching into the hole, Harper loosened the trunk from the grips of its tomb, but the sheer weight of the trunk wouldn't allow her to lift it, only nudge it from the suction of the earth.

Emmett grinned. "Heavy is good." He looked just like the boy who'd dig for rocks and nonexistent fossils in the backyard. Once, they'd found an old Confederate Belgia bullet. Granddaddy had cleaned it up and displayed it in the shop until a collector had come to purchase it. He'd let them split the money. Emmett had spent all of his on this packaged gum that had trading cards inside. She couldn't remember what she'd spent her share on now.

Granddaddy stepped closer. "Get it up here."

Harper stepped into the hole and braced her footing against the sides that the shovel had scraped smooth edges against. Emmett reached in on the other side, and they lifted. Heavier than it looked, the trunk gave way from its nest in the dirt, and they set it rather unceremoniously on the unmarred grass to the side of the hole.

Sissy peered in close. "The lock's rusted."

With the shovel, Emmett snapped down on the lock. It bent with effort. Forcing the tip of the shovel against the rusted metal one more time, it gave way.

Harper sank down on the edge of the hole, anticipation causing her heart to quicken. She looked up at her granddaddy and nodded.

He sank down to his knees and pulled the box lid up; it stuck, creaking as a collective inhale passed between them.

Four heads bent over as the lid flipped back.

Harper's eyes immediately found Great Grand-mère's pearls, their opalescent sheen dull with a thin layer of accumulated grime. The string of pearls was wrapped around a ruby broach with grimy prongs that she'd once seen in a sepia photo of Grand-mère. Other trinkets were scattered about, a pile of silver and gold coins, inscribed with another language, and a folded glob of worn paper, not quite beyond repair, but close. A tarnished teapot rested on its side, covering other items.

Granddaddy reached in and his fingers fumbled beneath these layers, and Harper's breath caught as he pulled from the mass a gold bullion.

"And this, young people," Granddaddy said, "is why Grand-mère Amelia was livid but didn't let anyone know."

Sissy gasped, her eyes wide. "What in the world!"

Granddaddy handed it to Sissy, who handled it with such fear, it was as if he'd handed her a wild animal. "Her father sent her to America to be married and wanted to be sure she didn't suffer in what he believed to be a primitive area."

Granddaddy reached in, rummaged around, and pulled out another slightly dull gold brick. "She boarded a ship with five gold bars at seventeen years old to be married to her second cousin who she'd never met."

"Five?" Harper asked, peering closer into the depths of the

trunk. A little rusty on her gold prices, she knew enough about the value of gold to know that they had unearthed a small fortune.

Granddaddy continued, inspecting the gold bar. "Insulted, Grand-père Florian wouldn't allow her to use the gold. There may have been some animosity between the two families. The Ames have always been competitive, and the deal that had them married may have been part of a forced truce."

Harper's and Sissy's eyes met. Harper offered a lopsided grin to lighten the implication. They couldn't help that the competitiveness was in their genes.

Emmett accepted the bar Granddaddy handed him, moving it from hand to hand to gauge its weight. "So when the boys heard the soldiers were coming, they knew they were protecting more than pearls."

Granddaddy nodded. "Grand-père Florian didn't pay no mind for the most part because the boys didn't touch his wealth. He'd protected his own gold when the battles began popping up around Louisiana. Of course, ten years later the original house was damaged in a fire, and he really wanted that gold, having lost much of his wealth after the war. They didn't want anyone to know it was buried here, though. Plenty of nasty things could have gone on for someone to get ahold of something like this."

Harper searched his face. He seemed so alert, his thoughts so clear. Just like the man he'd been before the illness. Finding the treasure had sharpened his mind, even if it was momentarily.

Harper pulled the pearls out of the trunk, considering all the details Granddaddy had known that weren't in Ellis's journal. "You knew all of this?"

He grinned. "Ames family secrets. Decades to pull them out of my dad and paw."

Harper ran her fingers over the pearls, feeling the smoothness even beneath the layer of grime. "What now?"

"We wake your grams," he said, "and there's a bottle of champagne in the cabinet for the occasion."

Emmett

Wiping his brow with the back of his hand, Emmett closed the barn door, shutting the shovel away and ending the digging for the night. He felt sweaty and dirty, but if he stopped and got cleaned up, he may lose the momentum he'd built, or something might happen that could cause him to rethink his decision. It was now or maybe never in this grand, dramatic gesture.

From the ground near the foot of the chicken fence, he grabbed the old box and walked toward the kitchen light spilling onto the back lawn. Thirty or so minutes ago he'd watched Sissy and Harper, weighted down by the trunk between them, walk toward the house laughing and carrying on about needing to lift weights. He'd bowed out, claiming he had to take care of something quick, promising he'd be there shortly.

Digging up that old piece of construction paper had taken longer than he'd thought. Winston had come into his room and thought he'd gone crazy, as he'd torn through old boxes stuffed in the back recess of his closet. Since he'd not packed his childhood items away himself, he'd scattered them around the room to locate the map. Now his room looked like it had during boyhood. After locating it in a box of old drawings and notes from school, he'd run out trying to make up for the minutes that had ticked by.

Letting himself into the backdoor, he observed the celebration scene around the table before they noticed him. Clear plastic disposable cups had been filled with bubbly liquid from the black champagne bottle on the table. The trunk rested in the center of the table, its items spread out on a white, makeshift tablecloth.

As he moved past Mrs. Patsy's rocking chair, it creaked forward causing Harper to glance toward him. The excitement of the night had loosened the remaining tension in her face.

Harper motioned with her hand for him to join them. "You're missing the celebration. What were you doing?"

Emmett looked toward Walter and Patsy who were huddled together, smiling as Mr. Walter fiddled with a doubloon from the trunk. Sissy paid him no mind as she handled the items, critically inspecting each.

"I had to dig up some more treasure tonight."

Harper tilted her head, her eyebrows scrunching into her puzzled look. "What treasure?"

Emmett pulled the box to the front and opened the worn, slightly cracked chest and retrieved the bubble gum machine ring from inside.

"Harper Ames." He took a deep breath, feeling doubt nibbling at the edges. "I promised you that I'd return this ring to you one day."

Sissy's chair scrapped against the floor as she pushed herself back. "Oh my lord."

Emmett could only stare into Harper's emerald eyes, eyes that revealed a strange combination of fire and vulnerability right now as they looked into his. "I know I screwed up and wasn't there for you. Let's just say I was stupid back then, and I had to grow out of being an Hebert. I'm giving you back your ring now with a promise that if you give me a second chance, I promise I will always be there for you."

He burned beneath the intensity of her gaze. Then she laughed, tears brimming at the corner of her eyes.

"I will look funny wearing that ring."

His heart swelled. He couldn't believe this crazy idea had worked.

Dropping the box and pulling her into him, he felt her softness mold to his body. Leaning forward, he gathered her lips into his, feeling the passion instantly. It was better than his head had built it up to be.

Clapping interrupted moments later, and they pulled away, embarrassed.

Harper leaned her head into his chest, squinting her eyes closed, hiding a chuckle against his shirt. Emmett looked toward the table where their audience looked on.

Mrs. Patsy smiled. "More than one treasure for this family tonight, I'd say."

Two Months Later
Harper

Wiping the glass down, she scrutinized the case for any hidden fingerprints. She stood back and stared into the glass, trying to place herself as an objective observer. The gold bars gleamed in a pyramid style centerpiece. Grand-mère Amelia's pearls, delicate and opalescent, lay beautifully across the black velvet, framing an intricately jeweled hair comb. The silver-plated tea service, now polished and restored, gleamed from its tray. The Napoleon coins were sprinkled across the velvet, but they were placed so the inscription could easily be deciphered. Not bad for a display, if she did say so herself. None of it had a price tag, but Granddaddy had loaned them to her to draw attention and to get patrons into the doors.

Harper scanned the shop. After extensive cleaning and tossing out, she'd revamped the antique store. Repainting the walls and updating the lighting and fixtures had gone a long way in transforming the store into an upscale antique haven instead of a thrift store. Ames Antiques now had its third generation owner, and she didn't want it to fail.

Today was the day of reckoning though. The grand reopening.

The door swung open, and Emmett strolled through carrying a French cane chair they'd discovered at a flea market this past weekend for a steal. Sanding and varnishing it had brought back memories of her mother, and, for the first time, they weren't marred by sadness.

Emmett glanced around the store. "Back corner?"

She came around the corner of the case to meet him. "I think so."

He set the chair down and pulled her roughly toward him, kissing her. He'd shaved this morning, so her fingertips brushed the smoothness of his cheek, intensifying that ember in her chest that always burned at the thought of him.

"You two need to get a room." Sissy walked toward them, her hands filled with an oversized tray of desserts.

"Won't we have one soon?" Harper smiled, leaning into Emmett's chest. He'd spent more time in the outdoors, and she thought the smell clung to him now. It fit him.

"Yeah, yeah, yeah," Sissy said, shaking her head. "I will have everything out of the house tomorrow."

Emmett ran his hand over her arm. "And your house, well apartment, warming party?"

Harper bit down on her lip, covering the smile that had risen to her lips. They'd planned a surprise for Sissy, and Harper was having a difficult time not spilling the secret. Emmett's hand had been a warning, but not a good enough one.

Sissy looked at Harper, her eyes narrowing in on her reaction. The woman was a keen observer. "Next weekend. And you two are bringing the wine as promised."

Harper nodded. "Whatever you need."

Oh, they'd be bringing Sissy's new wine collection and a friend who'd offered to build her the storage as well. But Harper couldn't say that just yet.

"Of course, it's me moving out so that you two have a house." Sissy frowned, but there was a sparkle in her eyes.

Harper laughed. "Oh, be still. You couldn't wait to move back into this building."

Sissy put her hand on her hip, which was her signature move. "You got that right. Less grass, dirt, bugs, and everything else I don't like."

Emmett squeezed Harper's arm. "Are you ready?"

Harper bit down on her bottom lip. "I think so."

Sissy threw her hands in the air. "Of course you are. We Ames women are in charge now. We need to let the rest of the family know when Grams and Granddaddy are here, though. Granddaddy says the cousins are coming from Shreveport. Do we like them? I can't remember."

She squinted her eyes, thinking about it.

Harper shrugged. "As Grams would say, they are northern people now. They might as well come from another country."

Sissy tilted her head. "Well, I like you two, but that's probably about it. And no offense Emmett, but you are going to be an Ames one day. You belong to this family. About time you had our last name, since you are essentially an orphan."

Emmett looked down on Harper, his eyes warm with laughter. Sissy would always be Sissy, after all. But he'd been right; life was better when the three of them were a team. Sissy's phone buzzed and she glanced down at the offending object in her hand. "Granddaddy's here."

Harper exhaled. It was time to open the doors.

Enjoyed the book? Please leave a review where you bought it.
Help spread the word!

ALSO by JESSICA TASTET

The Raleigh Cheramie Series

THE CUSTOS SAGA

JESSICA TASTET is the author of five novels including the Raleigh Cheramie series. She lives in southern Louisiana with her husband and children. For upcoming new releases visit her website at **www.jessicatastet.com**

.